D0920921

Salt and Light: Twenty-Five Days for Making Life Matter

By

Shane Stanford, M.Div.
Ronnie Kent, M.D.

PRESS

STEVE -
YOU ARE SALT
& LIGHT - KEEP IT
UP
RONNIE
CPH 3:20 &21

Salt and Light
by Shane Stanford, M.Div. and Ronnie Kent, M.D.

Printed in the United States of America

Library of Congress Control Number: 2003091640
ISBN 1-591606-79-9

Xulon Press
www.xulonpress.com

To order additional copies,
call 1-866-909-BOOK (2665).

Table of Contents

Week Two: Wait

Week Three: Witness

Week Four: Worship

Introduction

By
Shane Stanford

1986 was an important year for me. I was sixteen years old and had no idea that I was at a crossroads in my life. Three events took place that changed me forever, and sent me down a road of faith, doubt and discovery. For it was in 1986 that I began dating the girl that I would eventually marry, preached my first sermon, and discovered that I was HIV positive, contracted from contaminated medicine used to treat my Hemophilia. It is difficult to express the roller coaster of emotions of that year. But, more than that, the eventual profoundness of those events converging in my life was overwhelming. Looking back now, I see God's hand at work in the midst of joys and sorrows, pain and great excitement; and I see that He has never failed. My life has been a living miracle for more than one reason; and, beyond the struggle, I thank God for the journey. My hope is that the following devotional guide will give you a glimpse not only into my life, but also into the power of God to transform the disappointments and celebrations of this world to a means of eternal significance.

This project began as a devotional series for Advent. Hence, there are twenty-five Devotions (including the one for Christmas day). Advent derives from the Latin word, meaning "to come." It is a season for preparation and discovery. There is a completeness to Advent that makes it unique in the Christian calendar, for it focuses on both the birth and second coming of Christ. In the process, those who celebrate Advent are encouraged to address their own hearts and lives and to be available for God's grace. This grace is not just for the Christmas season, but can—**and should**— be lived out each day in our faith. The coming of Jesus teaches us that our lives matter to God and, at the very least, should be lived in a way that they matter to us as well.

As you can tell, this project has evolved into something much more than just an Advent devotional. Somewhere along the way, it became personal—not just because of the time and energy put into its development, but because of the nature of the work. I have written short stories, term papers and editorials before but never anything like this. Devotionals are different. They are meant to inspire, inform and inflame. But, they should also lead somewhere, and bring some fun along the way.

This is not your "grandmother's" devotional guide. The stories are not always reverent, and they are often void of deep theological ramblings. But, hopefully, they encourage the reader to think about the power of faith and the journey that can lead them there.

If you have ever attended Asbury Church, you know why I chose the title, *Salt and Light*. It is our church family motto, and we say it after every Sunday service. But, I also wanted to express the sweet nuance of the Gospel to both enlighten and amuse. Jesus' message changed the world, but it also gave it some spiritual flavor. And, along the way, He taught us to value ourselves as God values us and then to share that with others.

Using this guide is simple. The weeks are divided into themes (Watch, Wait, Witness and Worship). Each theme points to a particular principle for the day. At the end of each day's Devotion is a journal focus to assist in your quiet times. I encourage you to not only read the Devotions, but to spend some time with the *Growing Deeper* and *Checklists* sections written by Ronnie Kent. Ronnie is a pediatrician by trade and a minister of the faith by heart. He also happens to be my spiritual mentor and discipleship partner. As you read in his introduction, Ronnie is the one who coined the phrase "be salt and light," and the one who taught me how important this simple process is to faith. The *Growing Deeper* sections will provide tools for deepening your spiritual walk.

But, above all, I hope you enjoy the journey. I believe that real growth happens over time and is perpetual. So... boldly go where God leads.

On a personal note, I want to say thank you to those who helped tremendously by editing and critiquing the project. Thank you especially to Patty Ward for her diligent editing and guidance. Your help has been immeasurable. Barbara Loper, Lisa Ziz, Kelli Phillips and Jill Burgess were helpful in making sure that my crazy prose didn't get out of hand. Thanks for keeping me straight.

To my mom, Buford and Whitney, thanks for such a strong foundation and for enough love and support to accomplish anything, no matter the circumstances. Mom, I especially appreciate your journey—first, as a single mom who cared faithfully for a sick child, and second, for a witness that screamed your love for God. You will never know how that shaped who I am. I love you.

However, I especially want to thank Pokey, Sarai Grace and Juli Anna for being the reason why life means so much to me, and why I have never given up hope. You are my flavor and my inspiration, and I love you.

So, sit back and relax. Don't be too critical. Laugh, cry, whatever... but, above all, make it matter.

Shane

Taste and See …
A Primer for Making Life Matter

By
Ronnie Kent

"Be salt and be light" – my children have heard their mother and me say that to them since they started leaving the house to go into the world by themselves. That was usually followed by "The world needs you." We wanted them to know at an early age that they had a responsibility to make life better for the people in their world. We also wanted them to know they were not on their own. Not only were we always available, but more importantly, God was always with them. His presence, I believe, is the real key to our ability to make a difference in this world.

I am afraid that we often confuse the fact that Jesus has promised never to leave us with always being aware of His presence. It is simple but not automatic. I believe you have to read the Bible, pray, and love Jesus. Is this to earn His presence? No, it is to be aware of His presence. We read as if we were reading an owner's manual to a precious piece of equipment. We pray to be able to hear the whisper of His heart. And we love Jesus because He first loved us. If we are not going to be just like everyone else, we will need Jesus to help us.

A devotional guide should really be unnecessary. We should all have such a hunger and thirst for God's word that we read it often. But, that is usually not the case. Whether it is familiarity, hurry, or apathy, we just don't read like we should. This guide is just that—a guide to a real treasure, but not *the* real treasure. It is not a substitute for reading the Bible but hopefully a catalyst to do so. It should show you how significant a time with God is in other people's lives and stimulate you to do the same.

The themes of this guide are watch, wait, witness, and worship – the natural progression of our relationship with God.

We wait on God. No matter how hard we try, we cannot do anything without Him. He promises us that. We ask, and we wait. We wait like we wait for that child to come home on the bus after their first day of school. We wait like we do for a child who has been off to college for the first time to drive up in the driveway. We wait. We beg God to visit us with His presence so we can be with Him and be like Him. We know ourselves and our limitations and know that we really can't do anything on our own. We wait knowing He will come to us. If you seek Me you will find Me, if you seek Me with your whole heart. We wait because we have no choice.

We watch for God. We watch where He is and go there to be in His presence. We watch like Jesus did. He said He only did what He saw His father doing. We watch like window people not mirror people. Too many times we only see the world as we have seen our own reflection in it. We judge everything by how it will affect us. We take up too much of the view. We also start to see more and more of our own faults and start to wonder how, with all of our faults, God could use us. What we need to do is see the world as Jesus did. He was always looking at others and their needs for He knew that His father would take care of Him— so why be concerned?

We witness. We just simply tell the truth about what God has done for us. Whoops. Now we've really gone and done something. I can wait on God, and I can watch for Him, but don't even think about me witnessing. I don't know how. I might offend someone. They might reject me. I get the privilege of seeing families of newborns. I can always spot the grandparents. They will talk to whoever happens to be standing by them at the window. They may not have even held their new grandchild, yet they are an authority on that baby. This may be their first grandchild and they don't even know how to grand-parent, but they talk anyway. Why, I have seen them keep talking when the person just turned and walked away. They do not care. You see, the reason they are talking is that they cannot help but talk. That is a part of them in that bassinet. That is their contribution to eternity. They are overwhelmed with love and joy, and it just overflows on to whoever is around.

We worship. That is just the natural outcome of God's presence. As we wait for Him with great anticipation, as we watch Him come to us, as we see Him move through us to affect our world around us, we worship. It just comes out as we tell Him how much we love Him; as we tell Him how great He is; as we beg Him to stay close to us. Enjoy, He does!

What Every Devotional Experience Requires

Consistency: Make sure that you are working faithfully through your devotional experience. Not every day will be the same, but it is important to stay the course and watch for God's work in your life.

Prayer: Every devotional experience must begin and end with prayer. This is true for the process as a whole and for the daily moments as well.

Life Objective: No devotional experience is complete without a specific life objective that encourages the participant to "live out" in the world what they are studying at home.

To Consider...

Is it really important to spend time with God each day?

Is it really important to eat each day?

Principles to Live By...

If you have a time with God each day to prove your devotion to Him, it will not work!

If you have a time with God each day to survive, you have what it takes to have a consistent time of significant bible study and prayer.

> "For from Him and to Him and through Him are all things. To Him be the glory forever!" Romans 11:36

Section One

Watch

Recognizing God's Presence

1 Corinthians 1: 3-9

Preparing Our Hearts

An Outline for a Deeper Prayer Time:

Many people use the Lord's Prayer (Matthew 6) as an outline for praying. The Lord's Prayer is divided into usable sections that help provide focus and consistency. They are:

Praise and Adoration: Our Father in Heaven, hallowed be thy name... *Always begin a prayer by praising God and being in His presence.*

God's Will and Work in the World: Thy kingdom come, Thy will be done, on earth as it is in Heaven... *Pray for God's will to be done in the needs and concerns of the world and its many situations.*

Our Basic Needs: Give us this day our daily bread... *God intends for us to ask for our needs in* this life; however, these requests must always be balanced against God's will in our lives.

Forgiveness and Restoration: Forgive us of our trespasses, as we forgive those who trespass against us... *Prayer is ultimately about renewal and new direction; however, one cannot do that unless we are able to address those broken relationships in our lives.*

Strength in Adversity and Temptation: And lead us not into temptation, but deliver us from evil... *God never intends for His children to be in harm or distress; however, in this world, we oftentimes find ourselves in those places. Pray for God's strength and wisdom to endure and prevail in these moments.*

Praise and Adoration: For Thine is the kingdom, and the Power, and the Glory, forever. Amen... *Always finish the prayer where you began, by praising God and being in His presence.*

To Consider...

Why do you pray?

Why did Jesus pray?

What do you expect to happen when you pray?

Principles to Pray By...

If the objective of your prayer is a thing or an event, you may often be disappointed.

If the objective of your prayer is the presence of God, you should never be disappointed.

"Delight yourself in the Lord and He will give you the desires of your heart."

(Psalms 37:4)

Devotion One: Watch…

For the Wonder in Creation

"You made the delicate, inner parts of my body and knit me together in my mother's womb. Thank you for making me so wonderfully complex! Your workmanship is marvelous— and how well I know it…"

Psalm 139: 13-15

Human beings are memory freaks— that is to say we are obsessed with memorable moments. One only has to watch Classic Sports Network or the History Channel to be overwhelmed with our passion for those events and situations that have changed, shocked or inspired us.

I, too, am a memory freak. I love to look at old pictures, talk about the "good ol'days" (whenever those really were) and reminisce about the "could have beens" in life. But, my favorite memories are the births of my daughters. My wife and I were told that, because of my health, we should never try to have children. Yet, through the power of modern medicine, we have two beautiful healthy girls. They are as different as *night* and *day*. Sarai Grace, the oldest, is quiet and docile. Her favorite color is pink, and she likes to play princess and have tea parties. Juli Anna is loud and loves to laugh. She likes to become a super hero and—literally—fly through the air. They are truly unique. But, each one has a special place in my heart.

As distinctive as they are, in my eyes they also share a common thread of wonder. For you see, I cannot think about the birth of my children without being in awe of God. To think that from a tiny spark of existence my two precious girls came into the world. And… from that same spark came everything that has ever been made.

For that is the wonder of creation— that as unique as we all are, we are held together by an unbreakable bond, our Creator. His care in crafting this world resonates through each of us. We see it in the oceans, the sky, the summer breeze; and we experience it in each other. The vastness and complexity of the universe cannot surpass the simplest human joy. A baby's first word, a couple's first special moment express a deeper sense of creation than just science— it is wonder.

During this time of faith and preparation, I would encourage you to think of the wonder of creation in your own life. Sure, there are differences in how we might experience it, but we can share in the similarities as well— our basic need for hope and to be loved. And... maybe along the way you could say thank you to the One who did the knitting.

Growing Deeper

Prayer: Gracious God, help me today to slow down and enjoy the beauty of Your creation, whether in the world or in the heart. Please don't let me miss the wonder of You all around me. Amen

Journal Focus: Make a list of the blessings that you see in Creation and in your life. Thank God for them.

To Consider...

Why are you like you are? Do you think God says "oops" when He creates some of us? I have children in my practice with devastating handicaps. Did God forget about them in the process of their creation? We have all been created in the image of God, yet none of us have His total image. Could it be that in all of our strengths and weaknesses we can somehow see the total concept of God? Do those with awesome ability contribute any more than those with awesome handicaps? Without people with needs, how could we experience the compassion of God flowing through us to them?

Devotion Two: Watch...

For Opportunities to Make a Difference

"Make the most of every opportunity for doing good..."

Ephesians 5: 16

C.S. Lewis once stated, "I believe that men of this age think too much about the state of nations and the situation of the world... In the poor man who knocks at my door, in my ailing mother, in the young man who seeks my advice, the Lord Himself is present: therefore let us wash His feet." (534)

Many people in the world wonder if they can truly make a difference. In helping people discover their spiritual gifts, I am amazed at how many believe they have nothing to offer in service to Christ.

Nothing could be farther from the truth.

In fact, each of us has been gifted to play an important part in what we Christians call the Body of Christ. In Ephesians 4:12, the Apostle Paul states that God gave us these gifts for "the building up of the Body" and to do God's work in the world. The ability to accomplish our task for Christ is limited only by our willingness to do so. Making a difference requires hard work, diligence, and—often times—sacrifice. But, more than anything, it requires awareness of needs, hopes and fears that rest in the hearts and souls of those around us. My best friend has that ability. Ronnie is a pediatrician whose skill at life is as potent as his skills as a physician. He has the unique gift of knowing that a person's heart or life is not well and responding with words of encouragement, guidance or kindness. Not a child or parent leaves his office without knowing that someone cares, and that at least one person in this world will be praying for their situation. One of Ronnie's greatest spiritual gifts is awareness.

Jesus' ministry was definitely filled with an awareness of the myriad of opportunities for making a difference. The Scriptures are full of stories in which Jesus changes hearts and lives by simply being present and being Himself. Whether it was a blind beggar, a prostitute or a synagogue leader, Jesus was always willing to listen, touch and heal. In a world where we so often wonder *how* we can play a significant role for goodness, maybe we should stop and see that those opportunities are all around us.

Growing Deeper

Prayer: Gracious Lord, give me the serenity of heart to see the places in my world where I can serve others for You. Help me to see that in each opportunity You are present. Amen

Journal Focus: Write down the places in this world where you are currently serving God. If you can't list any, then make a list of places where you will begin serving.

To Consider...

Are there people with needs in your world? I feel quite sure the answer is yes!

Why is it we don't minister to those people more? Could it be that we are so worried about our own well-being, or should I say survival, that we have little time for the needs of others? Why was Jesus able to constantly minister to others? I believe He was so secure in the presence of His Father that He had all His time for others. I want you to try a little experiment based on a sermon of a previous pastor of mine. If God moves you, take a little time to inquire if the person you ask, "How are you doing?" is really doing "Fine."

Devotion Three: Watch...

For "Behold" Moments

"The next day John saw Jesus coming toward him and said, "Behold, there is the Lamb of God who takes away the sins of the world. He is the one I was talking about...""

John 1: 29-30a

I am a recent convert to the world of insomnia. Hours of staring at the ceiling have now given way to incessant television watching and Internet surfing. I have discovered that one can find the cure or answer to just about anything on late night television. The buffet of infomercials is overwhelming; yet, because of them, bald people can find hair, too hairy people can find more skin, and any poor fellow with a bad goatee and $79.99 can learn how to be a millionaire. It is not a pretty picture.

However, recently, my late night television watching habits have been transformed by one single channel— CSpan. I am captivated by the BBC's (British Broadcasting Company) political coverage. We think our politicians have quirks... Oh, no, my friend! I particularly enjoyed watching the opening of Parliament and the State of the Commonwealth address by the Queen. I especially appreciated her introduction. A rather rotund man bangs on a large, locked door and screams at the top of his lungs, "Behold, her majesty, Elizabeth, Queen of England, Ruler of Great Britain, Sovereign of the Commonwealth, Mother of the Most dysfunctional family on earth..." or something like that. Adding to the uniqueness of the scene is that the locked door on which the man is banging had just been slammed in his face for theatrical emphasis. The entire drama is fascinating; but, in actual British politics, it is little more than *good show*. As with our political system, most important decisions are made behind closed doors. But, I like the pageantry because it is a "behold" moment. You know what I mean, moments when we stop because something special is about to happen.

The above scripture passage is a great behold moment. John had been preaching diligently about the coming of the Messiah, and, right in front of him— there He is! He had to have been so relieved; everything that he had promised the people was happening.

Behold moments are more than just "made for television"; they are when promises are answered, when lives are transformed, when God's presence is more real than ever.

Over the past few weeks, I stopped and watched for *behold* moments, and guess what? I found plenty of them. And… God likes them. No, I mean he really, really likes them! Not because they are always flashy or bold (sometimes they are rather subtle), but because in those moments, He has our attention.

Every time a person is baptized, I have a behold moment. When a marriage is put back together or made healthier, I have a behold moment. When the Body of Christ really acts like it, I have a behold moment. They are all around us, and they are wonderful.

So… for the insomniacs of the world, may I suggest a 1:00am info-session on the world famous Juice-a-matic. But for all of us, I hope that we will never sleep spiritually through those moments when God seeks to announce, change and amaze. "Behold, the Lamb of God…." Wow!

Growing Deeper

Prayer: Gracious God, thank You for being all around me everyday, and for wanting me to see Your presence in this world. Help me to not miss those moments when you are doing amazing things so that I might soak them up and become a witness to Your grace. Amen.

Journal Focus: Make a list of the "behold" moments that you witness today and for the next several days. How was God revealed in each of them?

To Consider...

What do you see when you see Jesus walking toward you? Is your first thought of fear or excitement? Do you want to walk with Jesus just for yourself? When John told the people to "Behold," do you think they all stopped what they were doing, or did some miss that the Savior was there? When we behold Jesus, don't be surprised if He has someone walking with Him that may need our touch.

Devotion Four: Watch...

For Injustice and Unfairness

*"The Lord gives righteousness and justice
to all who are treated unfairly."*
Psalm 103: 6

My six-year-old daughter hates injustice. I am not sure that she necessarily understands the word, but I am convinced that she understands the concept. In her world, no one should cry, be alone or be hurt. And... absolutely no one should be forgotten. To a child—or to an adult— injustice when it happens should not be hard to see or feel.

But, adults are so unlike children in many ways. Children wear their hearts on their sleeves, only to give them away. Adults... well, you get the picture!

How sad it must be for God to look down and see a world of grown-up children who have forgotten how to be appalled for righteousness sake.

In our busy world, we religious folk are too often consumed by the task of doing life that we often miss the meaning of it. And... in the process, we pass by countless individuals who believe the God we serve has forgotten about them.

In Mark 1: 40, a leper calls out to Jesus, "If you are willing, you can make me well...." And, what was Jesus' reply? "Of course, I am willing!" That passage has always struck me for its simple yet powerful lesson in caring about the plight of others. How many had passed by that leper before Jesus? Had anyone stopped? Did anyone care? And what was it about Jesus that made the man call out? Had he called out to others? Oh, so many questions!

The truth is that injustice, unfairness and leprosy of many forms are all around us. They are at the gate, in the living room, at work and in the back yard. They are even at church. Do we hear the cries? Do we dare notice? Are we bold enough to stop? If the Lord gives "righteousness and justice to all who are treated unfairly," what about the ones who do it to them? Even worse, what about the ones who see it, but do nothing?

Growing Deeper

Prayer: God of Grace, please forgive me for when I have not responded to injustice and unfairness in my world. Help me to resolve those matters that I can influence, pray for those that I cannot, and always point to You as an alternative to the situations of this world. Amen.

Journal Focus: Make a list of areas of injustice within your world that you can affect today. What steps should you take in order to address these issues?

To Consider...

Why does injustice occur? Why does God allow it? Don't you think that if you were God you would at least *zap* someone a little when they hurt someone else? Do we ever think God himself is unjust? Why is a mother killed by a drunk driver or a young child maimed in a drive by shooting? The questions can reach a paramount, but I know God is never surprised. He never nods off or goes on vacation. God is fully aware of injustice because He has experienced it. The greatest injustice that ever was took place when Jesus was nailed to that cross for my sins and yours. And yet, God watched and did nothing. Just imagine. When Jesus looked down at that man holding the hammer, He asked His Father to forgive him.

Devotion Five: Watch...

For Signs of Community

"They joined with the other believers and devoted themselves to the apostles' teaching and fellowship, sharing in the Lord's Supper and in prayer. A deep sense of awe came over them all, and the apostles performed many miraculous signs and wonders. And all the believers met together constantly and shared everything they had. They sold their possessions and shared the proceeds with those in need. They worshiped together at the Temple each day, met in homes for the Lord's Supper, and shared their meals with great joy and generosity all the

> *while praising God and enjoying the*
> *goodwill of all the people. And each day*
> *the Lord added to their group those who*
> *were being saved."*
>
> **Acts 2: 42-47**

The church had experienced troubles for many years. Generations of bad choices, harsh words and dissolved relationships had obviously produced a very dysfunctional system. The spirit of unrest palpitated from the first moment that I entered the place. It was their revival time, and I was charged with the job of doing it. Over time, *revival* had come to mean four days each year when the guest speaker arrived to preach about sin. Covered dishes reigned, and everyone pretended to get along. When the revival was over, things quickly returned to normal. It was a pattern to which this family of God had grown accustomed.

My arrival was full of quirks and mistakes from the start. First of all, I was mistaken for the copier repairman instead of the preacher. Once they were satisfied that I was indeed old enough to lead the revival, an older, wiser gentlemen and lady of the church proceeded to orient me on the needs of this congregation. "We need to hear about sin, and how people should change their ways. These 'young people' just don't have any respect...." I am almost sure that no audible alarms went off, but I can't guarantee it. It was one of the saddest moments of my ministry.

For the next four nights, I preached on sin, but

not their understanding of it. No, instead, I talked about biblical community, and how God intended for the Church to be His representation, not just of his work in the world, but of His very life. And... I preached that when we fail to be community, we fail God.

Acts 2 is about *community,* plain and simple. The scripture says that the very first church "joined together" and "experienced awe...." When is the last time you experienced awe in church? There was no mention of committees, by-laws or orders of worship, just brothers and sisters in the faith doing life together. They became a living expression of the person of God.

John Dewey writes, "What the best and wisest parent wants for (his/her) own children, that must the community want for all its children." I believe that God wants us to experience the connection that He experiences in the Trinity. The community of the Father, Son and Holy Spirit is conspicuous. It is the very best expression of intimacy and existence that our humble minds can understand.

God chooses this for the church so that through this community, we become what we were created to be—the children of God, together.

Growing Deeper

Prayer: Gracious God of all, help me to be bound to Your body and to work for its health and strength in all that I do. I pray that, along with brothers and sisters in the faith, You will be seen in all that we do and that it will make a positive difference in the world. Amen.

Journal Focus: If you belong to a body of believers, make a list of areas within the church where you can have a positive effect. What areas of negativity can you address? If you are not a member of the body, make a list of the reasons why— then resolve to find a community where you can share your faith and grow.

To Consider...

What, or who, keeps the church of today from being a church of true "Acts 2" community like that of the first century? In Jesus' prayer in *John 17*, His request for the church is "may they be brought to complete unity to let the world know that you sent me and have loved them even as you have loved me." Could it be that one of the reasons that the world struggles with the reality of Jesus is that the church struggles with the reality of unity? Could it be that the key to unity is as simple as asking God to help us apply to our lives a little principle called the "Golden Rule"?

Devotion Six: Watch...

For the Adversary's Snare

"You won't die! The serpent hissed."
Genesis 3: 4

I am not a hunter... (and I have not played one on television). In fact, no one could be more removed from that world than I. However, a couple of years ago a friend took me to his hunting club to check on the food plots. Of course, I had no idea what these were, but I quickly realized that they existed to sucker unsuspecting deer to the shooting area by using their need for food. Wow! Who knew that eating could get you killed? (Unless, of course, you have watched any of the *Godfather* trilogy, but that is another devotional....) When you think about it, the idea is brilliant: use the animal's basic needs and instincts to entrap it.

The idea is not original. Anyone ever read Genesis 3? The serpent introduces Eve and Adam (yes, that is awkward sounding) to the concept of *self-will* and, through it, the failure of humanity. Poor Eve, poor dumb Adam... they never knew what hit them!

Unfortunately, the adversary is still at it today, and he uses the same old material. Why would he need something new when the original works so well? Most of our disappointments, failures and shortcomings are a result of this trap. I have never met a person who gets up one morning and says, "Today, I will screw up my life!" (Well, maybe Ralph the barber, but he was never quite okay.) Life destruction should never be a conscious choice. That said, why do we so often find ourselves caught in the junk of life? My theory is that we have a little help. The scripture tells us that the adversary "prowls the earth looking and watching..." To make matters worse, he understands our weaknesses and knows how to exploit them.

Jesus, in the Lord's Prayer (Matthew 6: 13), entreats the Father to "lead us not into temptation." This has always been a curious verse to me. Would God purposefully do that to God's children? No, but through our basic needs and desires, we often do it to ourselves. And... the adversary is glad to give us a little shove. I believe that Jesus is saying that when we walk with him, he can show us the traps, even when they look appetizing and inviting.

Several years ago, I was offered the chance of lifetime in the form of a career change. It would have meant more money and greater opportunities for advancement. Everything seemed perfect until I began to count the number of days I would be away from home and my family. The money and prestige began to pale in light of missing my daughter's first word or first scraped knee. A future full of earthly rewards didn't seem that appetizing sacrificed on the altar of my family.

We must watch **where** we are in this world as much as **what** we are doing in it. Remember, "All that glitters is not gold." In fact, it might be a food plot at the EZ Catch Hunting Club. Run, Bambi, Run!

Growing Deeper

Prayer: Gracious God, protect me today from myself and where my selfish desires will lead. Help me to focus on You and to trust that You will guide me far from those snares that Satan has planned. Amen.

Journal Focus: Make a list of patterns in your life that are destructive or unproductive, and must be changed.

To Consider...

Who among us does not want to "be like God?" I would hope all of us who claim to be His children seek after such purpose and righteousness. That was Satan's promise to Eve if she ate the fruit. So what was the problem? Eve chose to be like God her own way, not the way God planned for it to happen. I often am a very easy prey for Satan because he agrees with my plans and tells me to "go ahead, it will make you **happy** or it will help your family or friends, so just go ahead and do it, God won't really mind." Unfortunately, it ends up not being God's plan, and I find out that the *green, grassy spot* was planted over the septic tank all the time. "There is a way that seems right to a man, but in the end it leads to death." (Proverbs 14:12). Fortunately, God gives us a great alternative: "Trust in the Lord with all your heart and lean not on your own understanding; in all your ways acknowledge Him, and He will make your paths straight." (Proverbs 3: 5-6)

Devotion Seven: Watch...

For Moments of Goodness

"In the beginning God created the heavens and the earth. The earth was empty, a formless mass cloaked in darkness. And the Spirit of God was hovering over its surface. Then God said, "Let there be light," and there was light. And God saw that it was good. Then he separated the light from the darkness."

Genesis 1:1-4

In case you didn't know it, James Taylor is smooth. I don't mean cashmere sweater smooth, I mean... well, smooth. Even ugly men start to look good when James is working his magic. When I have finished listening to James belt out his notes of wonder and reflection, I pause and think, "That was good."

In fact, when I consider it, many *good* moments exist in this world. For instance, Smoothies are good. Sportscenter is good. Shania Twain is good. The Golf Channel is **very good.** Walking with my wife by the ocean at sunset, well… better than good.

I believe God enjoys His children experiencing *good* moments. As you can tell, my definition of *good* is not viewed in reference to a *bad*. Don't get me wrong, I do believe in the concept of *bad*. One only has to read my poetry from the 5th grade to understand it. No, I mean *good* as a way of representing God's presence in our midst. Like the word "love," you can't really explain it, but you know when it happens.

When something is good, I feel it and want more of it. The power to capture these moments is both gratifying and defining. As I mentioned earlier, sunsets are important to me. They are God's punctuation on the day. I can only wonder if, on that first day of creation, when God finished His work, He looked back and said, "Wow, not bad, that is good!" Then… He gave the day a sunset so that others could see it too.

A great deal has happened since that first day of Creation. The world has taken some pretty difficult turns and twists, and we don't always get it right. But, we still have sunsets, and that is not an accident. The good moments of life remind us that God has not given up on this world.

When John the Baptist saw the Messiah, the

Lamb of God coming down the way to be baptized, he must of thought, "This is good."—Chocolate cake, bubble bath, a morning kiss from your daughter— *good*. And, in that moment, it was worh it. The camel's hair, the locusts, the crazy Pharisees —everything became worth it.

Maybe we should spend more time with these kinds of moments instead of being consumed by the tough ones. Oh, I don't mean to belabor the trials of this world, for Jesus admits that "in this world" troubles exist. But then, he counters with, "Take heart for I have overcome the world" (John 16: 33). And... I believe that he would add, "I have seen the best and worst of it—and I still believe it is **good**."

The tough moments are balanced by children laughing, by the sun rising and setting, by beautiful music and by husbands and wives gazing into each other's eyes remembering the first time that they said, "I love you." **And it is good**... very, very good. Thank God.

Growing Deeper

Prayer: God of all good things, thank You for showing me the wonder of Your world and work. Help me never to take for granted those moments, places and people that make my world so special. Amen.

Journal Focus: Make a "Goodness" chart by listing the exceptional things in your life. Be sure to thank God each day for them. Make a list of those moments and places that we have never noticed as being good before.

To Consider...

Do you ever feel empty and formless? How do we get that way? I think by doing nothing. How do you define *good*? If it is only from your perspective, you may miss some of the best times in your life. In Matthew 7:11, Jesus said, "If you, then, though you are evil, know how to give good gifts to your children, how much more will your Father in Heaven give good gifts to those who ask Him!" As parents, most of us think that one of the best things we can give our children is a good education, but how many 13-year-old boys thank their parents for allowing them to go to school each day? Trust God that when we know something is right, it is also good; and ask Him to help you enjoy it. The real sticky thing is to also trust God when it doesn't seem right. However, this is how He can use our lives to make us more like Him. By trusting that God is always at work in and through us, we start to fill up and take on the very form of the One who created us. "For it is God who works in you to will and to act according to His good purpose." (Philippians 2:13). "We know that in all things God works for the good of those who love Him, who have been called according to His purpose... to be conformed to the likeness of His Son." (Romans 8:28-29)

Checklist

A Devotional Method for Spiritual Waiting:
Waiting on God to work and move in our lives is not easy. The following method can help provide a disciplined approach to patience for our daily walk.

1. **Daily Prayer and Study:** Take some time to be in devotion each day. At first, pick a schedule that is conducive to your lifestyle.
2. **Covenant Experience:** Develop a weekly opportunity for covenant and discipleship with friends or spiritual peers. This will promote accountability and spiritual growth.

3. **Servant Ministry:** Provide an opportunity for service beyond your daily routine.

This will help put some "hands" to your faith and grant you perspective.

Section Two

Wait

Being in God's Presence

2 Peter 3: 8-15a

Devotion Eight: Wait

In Prayer

"Keep on asking, and you will be given what you ask for. Keep on looking, and you will find. Keep on knocking, and the door will be opened."

Matthew 7:7

Everyone hates it. Young and old, men and women, religious and irreligious—you name it. Some may say that they don't, but I question their honesty. What am I talking about? *Waiting.* In fact, I am sure that somewhere in Academia there is a study that proves waiting can be hazardous to your health. (Especially, if you keep blowing your car horn at the big, burly fella in the late model Ford while driving on a dark two-lane road in south Mississippi.) *Waiting*—we don't like it in restaurants, on the road or in doctors' offices.

I think for many waiting signals non-productivity, loss of control or just down right laziness. In our culture, where time is money, waiting is bad business.

So why is it that God consistently requires us to wait? —waiting on answers, direction and healing. Lord, how many times do I need to pray for the diseases to be healed or for the anxious moments to cease? Sometimes, God's lack of response is seen as no response at all. Why does God so often employ the art of spiritual waiting in our lives? Well, why do parents want their children to wait before crossing the road, before taking the next bite of ice cream or swimming too soon after they have eaten? (The first two have to do with being splattered by a semi hauling hogs or by the worst "brain freeze" in the universe. I am convinced the last one is a myth!) Parents require waiting for our safety and (dare I say it?) for our own good.

I believe that *waiting* is too often equated with silence, or worse, inactivity. I am not talking about *silence*. Silence and waiting are not the same in Scripture or in the world. I differentiate the two this way: *waiting* is being still; *silence* is being still and going crazy. Personally, I love noise. Yes, I am one of those individuals who sleeps better with the television blaring. For someone like me, silence is a very disconcerting thing. In fact, I spent a weekend on a silent spiritual retreat only to end up sneaking out of the cabin to drive up to the local Stuckey's to find someone who would talk. I spent three hours conversing with a lovely gentleman by the name of Earl; we are still close.

No, *waiting* is something more particular than silence, and it is more intrinsic to the Christian walk. I believe it is similar to what Richard Foster, in his book *Celebration of Discipline*, calls "inner silence". And... according to my reading of it, God does not intend for it to be inactive or unproductive. In fact, Foster quotes Catherine Doherty who says "a day filled with noise and voices can be a day of (inner) silence, if the noises become for us the echo of the presence of God..." . What a relief it is to know that being quiet is not the same as being in God's presence. Rather, for me, waiting is about active listening.

In the above Scripture, Jesus tells his followers to be "active" in prayer. Most people think that prayer is a sedentary event that requires Mother Teresa-like acumen. But, to Jesus prayer was a powerful, productive experience whereby the children of God could see a little action in this world. Goodness knows that Jesus' audience needed some action, especially in the form of barriers broken down and hearts mended.

Jesus also knew that the power of prayer was not in the person praying, but in the One to whom it was directed. God will act, yes, but we must be willing to allow Him to respond in our lives in His timing. That is where *waiting* comes into the picture. "Keep praying, keep asking, keep knocking," Jesus said. But, let God be God. What a powerful concept.

And in that process, mountains can be moved, doors of oppression and suffering can be opened, and lost lives will be found. I can wait for that... On your mark, get set... watch God.

Growing Deeper

Prayer: God of never ending love, help me to actively wait on Your will and work in my life. Grant me patience to endure the struggles of this world and strength to make it so. Help me to trust Your timing in all things. Amen.

Journal Focus: Discuss areas of your life where you have been forcing your own will and solutions to issues instead of waiting on God's timing. How could waiting on God's will in your life have changed or could change those issues?

To Consider...

What does God use to decide if we have waited long enough? Is there some heavenly clock or does time even enter the picture? Does a living sacrifice decide how long it will be on the altar? One of my greatest lessons on waiting came from a most unlikely story – the Biblical story of Hanna. Hanna waited, begged, cried, and acted completely drunk with sorrow while asking God year after year for a son. The beauty of the story is that when her prayer was finally answered, her "song" was only about God and not a mention of her son was made. Could it be that the waiting is meant to develop a more intimate relationship with God, and time does not even enter into the equation at all? Is it possible, that the heavenly clock is heart shaped after all?

Devotion Nine: Wait...

For Fulfilled Promises

"And I am sure that God, who began the good work within you, will continue his work until it is finally finished on that day when Christ Jesus comes back again."
Philippians 1: 6

Her mother said to her, "Wait right here, I will be back in minute." But the little girl began to cry and followed after her. The mom turned to her little girl and said, "Sweetheart, wait right here. Mommy, will be right back." But the girl insisted, "What if you don't come back?" Mom, understanding the fear of her daughter, knelt down to her level, put her arms around her child and said, "Darling, has mom ever broken a promise to you?" The little girl whispered, "No." "Well..." mom said, "I don't intend to start now." What we have just witnessed is a "fulfilled" promise that has yet to happen.

Mommies don't break promises: neither does God. In his letter to the Philippians, Paul states that what God begins, He will complete. No questions, and no liability insurance needed. Why then, like the little girl in the story, do we often not trust the One who has yet to break a promise to us?

Maybe it is our natural fear of the unknown, the bogeyman under the bed and around the corner? Or maybe it is just our discomfort with putting our lives in the hands of others. But, is it possible to grow if we do not learn to have faith in promises?

Can a marriage survive if a bride or groom doesn't trust the covenant made to one another? Can children experience a true sense of identity if their hearts have been constantly abused and broken by the ones who are supposed to keep them safe? The answers, of course, are "no". Trusting in promises may be the most difficult, yet important, activity of our emotional lives. They are the foundation for our relationships and, even, for much of our self-esteem.

I believe that is why God has gone to such lengths to fulfill His promises in us and through us. He even became like us…. And, still, we struggle with trusting Him. But, God seems to understand our apprehension and, time and again, kneels by our sides and whispers, "Have I ever broken a promise to you? Well, I don't intend on starting now."

I am glad that mommies never break promises,

and that, occasionally, all children must be reminded of it. It paints a divine picture of a God who is so willing to fulfill in each of us, that which He was willing to give of Himself.

Lord, don't be gone long... but, for now, I will wait right here.

Growing Deeper

Prayer: God who never fails, thank you for loving me enough that You would go to any lengths to fulfill Your promises. Help me to trust in Your guidance and to know that You are working for the best in my life. Amen.

Journal Focus: Make a list of all your "fulfilled promises," then design how you are going to live those out in the world today.

To Consider...

When is a plum a plum – only when it is ripe or all the time? There is *a fulfilling of a promise* taking place in that orchard. If that little green, bitter orb hangs in there, it will one day be a big, fat, juicy, red plum. How do we hang in there as God is continuing His work until it is finished? Read your Bible, pray, and love Jesus. The plum just hangs there. Plums don't strain and grunt to grow; they just make sure they stay attached. That's what they concentrate on. The growing is someone else's job. "For no matter how many promises God has made, they are 'Yes' in Christ." 2 Corinthians 1:20. "Praise be to the God and Father of our Lord Jesus Christ, who has blessed us in the heavenly realms with every spiritual blessing in Christ." Ephesians 1:3 "I am the vine; you are the branches. If a man remains in me and I in him, he will bear much fruit; apart from me you can do nothing." John 15:5

Devotion Ten: Wait...

For Prodigals to Return

"So he returned home to his father. And while he was still a long distance away, his father saw him coming. Filled with love and compassion, he ran to his son, embraced him, and kissed him."

Luke 15: 20

When I was six years old, my dog, Blackie, ran away from home. (Yes, he was a black dog.) My mother tells me that I would wait every evening on the front porch for his return. At first, I would call out his name. Then, as time went by, I would just sit and wait. Eventually, I stopped waiting. I never really liked that dog.

I have a friend who has been "waiting" for her son to return for 30 years now. The son ran away from home in the midst of great turmoil. He had gotten into trouble with the law, was addicted to drugs and was constantly at battle with his family. One night, he left a terse note on his mother's kitchen counter and vanished. No word, no contact for 30 years. But... I know my friend; she will wait forever. She will never stop calling his name, and she will never take her eyes off of the horizon.

I wonder how long the father in Luke 15 had waited for his son. The scripture does not give us a proper timeline; it just says that "when the son had come to his senses," he went home. There must have been some agonizing days and evenings for that father. For we get the impression that he was most certainly waiting. The passage tells us that he saw his son "while he was still far off." Obviously, the father was paying attention to the horizon.

All of us have lost something important to us. After my high school graduation, I lost a $100 bill given to me as a gift. I looked all over the house, and, in the process, destroyed my room. I eventually found it (fallen behind a dresser). I was not giving up. It mattered to me.

The world is filled with lost things, and they break our hearts. But, God calls us to wait and watch, to not give up, and to not forget the horizon. If I will tear up a room looking for lost money, what will I do for a lost heart or soul? Will I give up on them because, unlike a dollar, I assume that they made a conscious choice to abandon that which I esteem? And, what if they did? Does that give me the right to forget them? God would say, "Absolutely not!" The story of the Good News is that God does not give up. He continues to wait, sometimes beyond hope, that one day we might "get it"—that we might "come to our senses" and make our way home. And guess what? He will be there waiting, and he will run to us and embrace us. He will do this because that is what people who have lost something do, and that is what all of us who are lost need. I have found that the same souls who scream at us, "Leave me alone!" are, deep down, really calling out, "but please don't give up on me."

One more thing, when the son comes home in Luke 15, the father throws a party. I am afraid that we do not party enough as Christians. Enough said.

Keep watching, keep your eyes on the horizon, and be ready to run.

Growing Deeper

Prayer: Gracious God, thank you for never giving up on me and for always seeking after my heart and life. Help me to care so much about my brothers and sisters that I, too, will seek, watch and wait for their lives to be changed in your grace. Amen.

Journal Focus: Make a list of those "prodigals" who need for you to seek and watch after them today. For those who have returned or will return, how can you celebrate what God is doing in their lives?

To Consider...

Why do you suppose the father did not go looking for his son? In fact, why did he not force him to stay at home in the first place? I think the second son is included in the story to answer that question. Sometimes people are lost but never go anywhere. They are lost because they have never been found. All of us need to have the sense of being looked for – of being important to someone. I think one of the saddest states of humanity is to feel completely unnecessary. Know that God is always looking for you, then look for someone, and watch the party begin.

Devotion Eleven: Wait...

For His Timing

"When Jesus heard that John had been arrested, he left Judea and returned to Galilee. But instead of going to Nazareth, he went to Capernaum, beside the Sea of Galilee, in the region of Zebulun and Naphtali. This fulfilled Isaiah's prophecy: "In the land of Zebulun and of Naphtali, beside the sea, beyond the Jordan River in Galilee where so many Gentiles live the people who sat in darkness have seen a great light. And for those who lived in the land where death casts its shadow, a light has shined." From then on, Jesus began to preach, "Turn from your sins and turn to God, because the Kingdom of Heaven is near." **Matthew 4: 12-17**

I am a channel surfer. I can watch fourteen different stations at the same time. It might be my spiritual gift. I especially enjoy a good commercial. Not that I am going to actually buy or use what they are selling, but I appreciate the high amount of creativity and boldness used.

Selling is big business, and these guys do it well. I have decided that it is true, they really could sell ice to Eskimos. But, we're also not talking about the parting of the Red Sea. After all, have any of you actually tried to eat frozen snow, pond or lake? I am sure that the Eskimos might enjoy some good ol' packaged ice every once in a while. But, I digress.

One of my favorite television commercials is the one about the guy with timing problems. Many of you have seen it. He is a few seconds off on everything. Worse yet, he's clueless about it. His tennis swing is a half-second off; his coin is too late being deposited in the tollbooth; and he loses his girl when his "I love you" comes just after the nick of time. It is not a pretty picture. This commercial drives home the point that timing is a critical part of life.

Waiting for God's timing does not mean delay, it means accuracy. The above Scripture talks directly about timing. For many, it is an often-overlooked passage, sandwiched between two important moments in Jesus' life. However, I believe that it is a critical moment for Jesus' ministry, because it is the moment when God's time for Jesus was apparent.

The Scripture states, "when Jesus heard that

John had been arrested… he went to Capernaum… and from that moment began to preach." Now, I have read this passage a hundred times and never noticed this point—Jesus' ministry had timing. He recognized God's will and knew that this was the moment to get started. Even in Jesus' life and ministry, there was a time for beginning something new.

Now, I don't believe this means that, prior to John's arrest, Jesus just sat around. From stories of his childhood, we know that he was very active in both his faith and vocation. Scripture tells us that people knew of him (John, for instance), and that He went to parties (weddings). He may not have been a social butterfly, but Jesus got out of the house regularly.

Jesus was not lazy, and he certainly understood timing. Many times, I get the two confused. My impatience in solving problems causes me to act too quickly, often making unwise decisions. I am a fixer. Overall, this is not a bad thing; but, at times, it can be a flaw. The Bible tells us "there is a time for everything under heaven." (Ecclesiastes 3: 1) There is a time to be born, a time to die, and even a time for the redemption of the world.

If God's timing is so precise, even in the sending of his Son, then shouldn't we believe that His timing is true for us? I don't believe that God is going to hide his plan from us when its moment of unveiling arrives. Jesus heard that John had been arrested, and he was convinced that this was the time. His patience, preparation, everything was now fulfilled. He was ready.

My prayer for each of us is that we might be ready and prepared when God's time is unveiled in our lives and ministries. When we force timing, we then have to spend valuable efforts cleaning up the mess. Watch for God's work, trust in His plan, and then wait for His timing.

You probably still won't get a commercial made about you, but you just might change your world.

Growing Deeper

Prayer: God of perfect timing, help me to trust in the ways that You work in and through me today. Thank you for being patient, but, above all, allow Your will to be realized that I might see the glory of Your presence today. Amen.

Journal Focus: List those areas in your life where you have not waited on God's timing. What were the results? What are some specific ways that you can show yourself and others about trusting God's timing?

To Consider...

Try the following works to deepen your spiritual walk and develop your spiritual timing.

Celebration of Discipline: The Path to Spiritual Growth by Richard J. Foster.

12 Steps to Living Without Fear by Lloyd Olgivie.

The Nature of Spiritual Growth by John Wesley.

They Found the Secret by V. Raymond Edman.

Living the Psalms by Maxie Dunnam.

The God You're Looking For by Bill Hybels.

If You Want To Walk On Water, You Have to Get Out of the Boat by John Ortberg

The Case for Christ by Lee Stobel

The Case for Faith by Lee Strobel

The Christian's Secret to a Happy Life by Hanna Whitall Smith

Devotion Twelve: Wait...

For a Hungry Heart

"God blesses those who realize their need for him, for the Kingdom of Heaven is given to them."

Matthew 5: 3

I have a passion for books. Two of my favorites are Max Lucado's *And the Angels Were Silent* and the *1999 General Minutes of the United Methodist Church*. They have some obvious similarities: they are bound; they are made of paper; they have pages and words; and, they have copyright licenses. In theory, these books are very much alike.

However, just look at the front cover and you can tell a difference. Lucado's book is colorful and soulful (not James Brown, but very intimate in spirit). *General Minutes* looks like a really bad, cheap cookbook. Lucado's book seems to speak, "Grab some cocoa and sit for a while." *General Minutes* screams, "Grab a bamboo shoot and ram it under your thumb nail, because that is the only way you will stay awake."

Open the cover and the differences only magnify. Lucado's book is a spiritual narrative that guides the reader through stories of hope and encouragement. *General Minutes* is filled with row after row of statistics and charts from every Annual Conference and every local congregation in the United Methodist Church. You would give your grandmother Lucado's work. You would hit her over the head and steal her purse with *General Minutes*.

Now, for those of you who have missed the metaphor, I would like to say two things. First, WAKE UP! Second, although both books are—well—books, that doesn't mean that they are the same on the inside. And, the insides define their nature.

This is true for human beings as well—especially Christians. Our outer selves can look one way, while our inner nature is something else entirely. The person who attends church because of status or obligation might look like everyone else, but something is clearly missing. That *something* is what I call a "hungry heart." In the above passage Jesus talks about those who hunger for God. They are the first ones mentioned in the Sermon on the Mount and are the inheritors of the Kingdom of Heaven.

It is clear from Scripture that Jesus was passionate, and He expected the same from those who would follow Him. Passion inspires, motivates and transforms our "insides" into a living narrative that tells of the wonder of God. But, as Jesus states, this hunger or passion begins with our need for Him.

Personally, I have to be careful about being so intent on doing good, Christian things that I forget to be a Christian in the process. The Kingdom is not given to the one who can present the strongest resume, but to the one who has no qualifications but a love for Jesus. A believer who does not have passion is as antithetical a concept as a person who performs a song beautifully but does not care about the words. As the old saying goes, church may make you stand up, but Jesus is the one who causes you to dance.

In my life and work, I am acquainted with many women, but I only have passion for one. Believe me, there is a difference. Don't judge a book by its cover, neither a heart.

Growing Deeper

Prayer: God of passion and presence, grant me Your heart today that I might live Christ in everything that I do. Help me to realize the difference of having You in my life and then help me share that difference with all I encounter. Amen.

Journal Focus: Make a list of the "dull" areas in your spiritual walk. How would they be different if infused with a sense of passion and expectation in

Christ? Example: Is your marriage or significant relationship filled with the passion of God?

To Consider...

10 Scriptures by which To Live with Passion:

1. John 3: 16-17
2. Mark 5: 36
3. Romans 8: 28
4. 1 Corinthians 15: 58
5. 2 Corinthians 12: 8-10
6. Philippians 4: 6-7
7. 1 John 1: 9
8. Ephesians 1: 11
9. Romans 10: 9
10. 2 Corinthians 5: 17

Devotion Thirteen: Wait...

For Self Control

"Knowing God leads to self-control. Self-control leads to patient endurance, and patient endurance leads to godliness."
2 Peter 1: 6

Gladys was the biggest, meanest person I ever met, and we met completely by chance. Gladys and I were witnesses to a traffic accident. No one was hurt and the damage was fairly minimal, but the nature of the accident made it difficult to tell who was at fault. Gladys and I had been shopping (separately) at a local convenience store when all the fun started.

Without giving all of the details of the accident, let me say that whenever an 83-year-old man in a Grand Marquis and a 16-year-old girl in a sports car decide to cross paths, the result cannot be pretty.

Thankfully, both of them walked away without a scratch (to their persons that is), but their cars were not so fortunate.

I learned in physics that with every action there is an opposite reaction. Well, when a Grand Marquis runs into a Miata, the reaction is, "Oh my goodness, that little car just got smashed." One can only imagine the pandemonium that began. Police, fire trucks and ambulances descended, cell phones blazed, and all the "rubber neckers" of the world (you know who you are) stopped and paid homage.

Now… back to Gladys. Gladys and I were the witnesses. The police officer, who was having difficulty understanding the details of the accident, turned to us for an explanation. As I normally do, I gracefully shared my thoughts on what I had seen, convinced that Gladys would agree. Gladys and I were apparently looking in different directions when the accident occurred. Her story, point by point, was the exact opposite of mine. The officer was not amused.

After I was able to collect myself, I simply said to Gladys, "I can't believe that we have such different views on this." Apparently, my words struck Gladys wrong, because she proceeded to put a "cussing" on me of which a longshoreman would be proud. It didn't take long to realize that Gladys did not care for me or, for that matter, any vertically challenged male. The dead giveaway came when she told me that I had a Julius Caesar complex. (I think she meant a Napoleon complex, but, to Gladys' benefit, I am not a fan of being stabbed repeatedly by my co-workers either.) Finally, the officer, who was five foot eight, stepped in and calmed Gladys down. He finished taking my statement, and I left. Gladys was still fuming.

A few weeks later, I saw that police officer at the mall. We immediately recognized each other. I stopped and asked if he had heard from Gladys lately; and, with a chuckle, he said, "No." But, then he proceeded to tell me how impressed he had been with my self-control. "Most people," the officer continued, "would have started hollering and arguing back, but you just stood there. It was impressive." (I didn't have the heart to tell him that it was simply out of fear of Gladys that I had remained silent.) I thanked him for his compliment and moved on.

However, as I have reflected on it, this presented a powerful opportunity for witness. Not, that I had to say the name of Jesus, talk about church or necessarily say anything religious. But…just because of my demeanor and my response, someone noticed and began to think.

How can a world that needs God see His presence? By seeing godliness in each of us. Peter tells us that "godliness comes from perseverance and perseverance comes from self-control" Yes, it matters *what* we say, but it is also important *how* we say it.

Growing Deeper

Prayer: God of grace, thank you for teaching me that being close to You requires that I experience

Your presence in my daily walk. Help me live life in such a way that my witness reflects You in all that I do and say. Amen.

Journal Focus: Make a list of the "Gladys" moments in your life. Could the situation have been different if you had reacted in a different manner?

To Consider...

"Some things in life are there for no other reason than to build your character."

My father has been the greatest human influence on my life. I was complaining one day when I was home from college about all the seemingly unnecessary aggravations of life when he made the above statement that I consider close to scriptural.

What part of 2 Peter 1:6 bothers you the most? There is no question for me—it's the "patient endurance" part. I want to have self-control and I want to be Godly, but I want it now!

Why does God put that "part" in so many aspects of the Christian life? You know, the "it takes time" part. When I gave my life to Christ I thought I became a new creation, created in the image of Christ. Well, an image may look like the original in some ways, but it is not the real thing. But, thank God, He has promised to work on me.

So why not instant Christ-likeness? I believe, once again, it is so we will need God. Patient endurance is a slow process, and we must stay in constant contact with God to achieve it.

"Some things" = Gladys?

Devotion Fourteen: Wait...

For Direction

*"You chart the path ahead of me and tell
me where to stop and rest. Every moment
you know where I am."*
Psalm 139: 3

Men and directions do not mix. We are not good at
following directions, and we certainly are not going
to ask for them. How many swing sets and bicycles
in this country today are operational in spite of a set
of directions? Fathers must receive a special dose of
grace every time a child swings through the air or
rides down the road. For most of us, directions are
for discarded pieces or for starting fires. (And all we
really need for that is two twigs and some gasoline.)

Trips are especially fun. Maps? Who needs
them? Give us the open road and an internal

compass. Oh, the places you can see when you really don't know where you are going! However, I have never heard a single man say that they didn't *trust* the directions for putting something together or in getting to some destination. No, the issue has always been with *following* them.

The Greek word "kateuthuno" means, "to make straight." It is also the equivalent of the English word, "direct." Another translation of the word, found in Luke 1: 79, literally means, "to guide." It is used over and over again in Scripture to distinguish God's guidance from the world's. In fact, unlike most Greek words, there is not a natural negative derivative of the word (ex: "un-direct" or "non-direct" do not exist). One can misdirect someone, but that is not the undoing of good directions; it is a conscious action from one person to another. No, in relation to the language of direction, one is either found or not found. It is that simple. Why is this important?

The laws of science states that the shortest distance between two points is a straight line. One either takes the shortest path or not. True, someone might detour and get to the same point, but the shortest path is still the shortest distance. It is a mathematical certainty—one of the natural laws.

Direction in our spiritual lives is the same. There are many paths that one can take, but only one shortest route. Scripture tells us God's guidance leads us on the easiest path to Him. The Psalmist echoes this by stating that God's intention is to make our paths straight and safe. It is more than wishful thinking; it is a biblical promise. For instance, the passage above shows us that God creates a map of our path and even shows us where "to rest." God deliberates and charts our direction. How amazing it is that the God of the universe cares about where I am going **and** how I get there!

How many of us have traveled difficult roads in our lives? Would a better plan or direction have made a difference? Of course! The struggle for human beings is not necessarily in *knowing* where we should go, but in *trusting* and then *following* the path to get there.

Growing Deeper

Prayer: God of the lost and found, thank you for always providing a clear path for me to follow. Grant me wisdom that I might discern it in my life and then have the courage to follow where it leads. Amen.

Journal Focus: Draw a "road map" of your life. Where could roads and choices "not taken" have led you? What made you choose the ones you did?

To Consider...

Why in the world do we not read the Bible more? It is *the* direction manual for life, and yet most of us are "hit and missers." Many tend to read the Bible only in times of need. Doing that is like trying to stay warm on a camping trip by lighting one match at a time. How silly, and yet that's what we do so often. Instead of taking the time to build a campfire that not only warms us and those around us, we just "get by" with scripture.

Is it any coincidence that the longest chapter in the Bible, Psalms 119, is full of promises that accompany being a diligent student of God's word? Please, read the Book, read the Book, read the Book! If you don't *I* can make you a promise. The front tire of your bicycle is going to fall off when you ride over some of the rough ground.

Section Three

Witness

Sharing God's Presence

Isaiah 61: 1-4, 8-11

John 1: 6-8, 19-28

Devotion Fifteen: Witness...

To a Fragile World

"For he has not ignored the suffering of the needy. He has not turned and walked away. He has listened to their cries for help."
Psalm 22: 24

In a recent article, Christian writer and poet, Steve Turner, discusses a conversation he had with U2 lead singer, Bono. In the exchange, Bono speaks about Christian music and the song, "Amazing Grace," in particular. This is what Bono said:

As a musician I am often struck by the phrase "sweet the sound" in Amazing Grace. I love to think that music can be an instrument of grace, that there might be mercy in melody and that at the very least a great song can fill the silence of indifference we sometimes find in our hearts (20).

Can a song fill the indifference of a heart? Amazing Grace was my grandfather's favorite hymn. He didn't just sing it; he sang it with *passion*. He sang it like the existence of gravity depended on the boldness of every note.

He said he liked the melody, but I think it was deeper than that. The words spoke to him. They filled a place in his heart that gave him hope and peace. He was especially transformed when he sang the phrase "that saved a wretch like me, I once was lost but now I am found, was blind but now I see."

My grandfather was a tough man who used his hands to build and fix things. No one would mistake him for soft or weak. But... when "Amazing Grace" crossed his lips, he was a fragile and vulnerable as a child. And, the very best of his strength and will were lost in the light of what God had done for him.

The calluses on our hands are nothing compared to those on our hearts. The witness of Christ to a fragile world speaks not only of grace, but also of the power of God entreating us to care and love again—to be made whole. Even the most "together" person has those tangled edges that do not heal alone.

Like the singing of a favorite hymn, a life touched by Christ is able to experience vulnerability again, and to believe, at least for one moment, that our souls *can* be heard. And, what do those hungry souls say? I believe that they are calling for a song, but not just any song—they want a song sung boldly, lived well and felt with passion. They want a song that matters; one that makes a difference. The human heart loves to sing, but can only be heard if the voice is lifted.

So, keep singing—and sing with passion. It will be a sweet sound to a fragile world.

Growing Deeper

Prayer: God of the sweet songs, thank you for placing a song within my heart that is your son, Jesus. Help me to sing and live His wonderful melody in my life with passion and purpose. Amen.

Journal Focus: Make a list of those areas of your life where God hears a song being sung today. What does God hear through the "music" of your life?

To Consider...

What type of music do you like? Classical, country, easy listening, pop? As Christians we all have our own unique song to sing. Each song is really no better or no worse than anyone else's song—just different. Why is that significant? Each person that does not know Christ or each person that has a unique hurt will respond differently to hearing another's unique song about what Christ has done for him or her.

I have heard people say that their testimony about what Christ has done in their life is simple and boring. They were not changed dramatically when they committed their life to Christ. They were not "saved" from some terrible wild life. To Christ, their song is just as sweet and just as useful as the drug addict living on the street. But, it is not just to Christ. To someone out there struggling to make it on their own skills and power, hearing that unique song could mean the difference in life and death.

The world needs *your* song. Not everyone will sing along with you. But trust me, if you keep singing, not only will someone eventually sing with you, some may even dance. Let the party begin!

"For we are to God the aroma of Christ among those who are being saved and those who are perishing."

2 Corinthians 2:15

Devotion Sixteen: Witness...

About a Free Gift

"God saved you by His special favor when you believed. And you can't take credit for this; it is a gift from God. Salvation is not a reward for the good things we have done, so none of us can boast about it. For we are God's masterpiece. He has created us anew in Christ Jesus, so that we can do the good things he planned for us long ago."

Ephesians 2: 8-10

If nothing in life is free, then why do Internet "pop ups" exist? Many, if not all of them, are advertising items and services that are free or can be free with the appropriate purchase. You can get free trips, free hotel stays, free air miles, free consumer counseling (that's irony), free loans, free everything… but money.

Most consumers don't believe in "free" things. Ask anyone on the street, and they will agree that "free" doesn't exist in our culture. However, our advertising speaks to something else—that we may not believe that "too good" is actually true, but we are more than willing to be convinced. Why is this? Because, in the mind of the consumer, no matter how you slice it, authentically "free" items cannot be bad.

Some friends of mine recently attended one of the "free vacations" about which telemarketers are always calling late at night. The catch was that in exchange for two nights and three days at resort on the Atlantic coast, my friends would attend a "brief" seminar introducing a particular company's new selling strategy. (This is short for pyramid scam.) After their brief orientation, my friends would be free to enjoy the amenities of the resort area.

Do I really need to finish this story or have you already seen the train to Suckerville pull away? My friends did not arrive at a five star resort (more like 2 1/2 happy faces). The accommodations were seriously lacking, the service marginal and the presentation lasted an entire day (eight hours). My friends left that evening, burned some Marriott reward points and soothed their bruised egos. They learned that, in this world, even free things have a price.

The real test as to whether something is actually "free" or not is in its value to someone else. Getting a free Mercedes might be a big deal in this world, while the kiss of a child or a cool spring day is taken for granted. Can you put a price tag on beauty? (And, I don't mean the $1 million in plastic surgery that Ivana Trump spent.) What about trips to the park, sitting on your grandfather's knee, or the birth of your child? What about forgiveness?

The apostle Paul, in the above Scripture, tells us that God's "special favor" in Christ comes to life in our faith. We cannot buy it, borrow it or steal it. It is a gift given freely from God's heart to ours. But, there is a catch. We must accept it and cherish it. Paul says explicitly that salvation is "not a reward for the good things we have done..." Instead, it is God's fulfilling of a future for you and me.

The passage goes on to mention that we are God's work of art—and not your run of the mill watercolor. Paul says that we are His masterpiece. A prominent artist once told me that patrons might purchase his artwork, but never the soul behind it. Each piece has an indelible mark of its creator imbedded deep within its nature, and no artist will ever give that up.

God is like that with us. He would pay any price and bear any hardship for His masterpiece, his soul of creation. For us, that is priceless.

Growing Deeper

Prayer: God of endless treasures, thank you for loving me so much that You consider me Your masterpiece. Help me to live in a way that pleases You and brings glory to Your name. Amen.

Journal Focus: Draw a picture of your life with a living story of your faith journey. Does this "masterpiece" reflect the presence of God's grace and work in your life? If not, why?

To Consider...

What do you do when you are given a special gift? Probably it really depends on the gift and—to some extent—on what the giver intended.

My wife loves to sew. When our children were younger she would spend hours— days making little dresses and suits for them. Her father saw how much she enjoyed this hobby and gave her a very special gift—a fancy, computerized sewing machine.

How do you suppose it would have made him feel if she had set that machine on our mantle and said, "This is so special I just want everyone who comes to our house to see it."? No, what makes her dad happiest is when he sees how she continues to work on that machine—sometimes to make those fancy little dresses (now for someone else's children), sometimes to repair a tear that was the results of a painful injury, and sometimes to make a pillow cover for a stinky ole dog. The fact that she is working this special gift is what pleases him.

So it is with our Heavenly Father. He loves to see us work out our salvation to make our world a better place. Plug yourself in – turn yourself on – and start "sowing." Whether it is to help God repair a tear in someone's life, make a dress to make someone feel special, or to help a stinky ole dog, let

Him pick the fabric and the use. Just stay at the machine.

"Continue to work out your salvation...."

Philippians 2:12

Devotion Seventeen: Witness...

To Bold Gestures

"Right away a woman came to him whose little girl was possessed by an evil spirit. She had heard about Jesus, and now she came and fell at his feet. She begged him to release her child from the demon's control. Since she was a Gentile, born in Syrian Phoenicia, Jesus told her, "First I should help my own family, the Jews." It isn't right to take food from the children and throw it to the dogs."

Mark 7: 25-30

Karen Hughes appeared to have it all. She had been the Communications Director and Principal Advisor to George W. Bush since his days as governor of Texas. In fact, the joke had been that Hughes had been by Bush's side since the "motorcade was just one car." It was an important and influential relationship. After his election to the Presidency, Hughes moved to Washington and immediately became a player on the national political scene.

You could not turn on the television for nearly two years without seeing her answering questions, dealing with policymakers and discussing the issues. She was tough, decisive and very much in control...or so it appeared.

Hughes would later state that, in spite of the fame and power, she had a hole in her heart. Her family had never been happy in Washington, and she and her husband had decided to move their teenage son back to Texas so that he could be "rooted" in a more stable environment. "My family is homesick," she said. And, in one the boldest moves in recent political memory, Karen Hughes gave up power to move home.

To the world, bold gestures can seem unthinkable. Why would someone give up power and fame for their family's sake, take a bullet for a friend, or give their money away to feed the poor? Why would a person willingly sacrifice the comforts of home to work in the wilderness, or eat the crumbs off the floor so that their children could be fed?

The woman that Jesus encounters in Mark 7 is on a mission. Her daughter is ill, and she believes that Jesus is the answer. As a Gentile woman, her willingness to confront Jesus, a Jew, is impressive enough. Women did not approach men in Jesus' day, especially when they were of two different cultures.

But, nothing was going to stop this woman from getting help for her child.

Her confrontation with Jesus is classic. Jesus uses the opportunity to teach the disciples about faith and, I believe, about gumption. His reply to the woman's request appears, at first, to be rather cold and unfeeling. "Why should I give the food of the children to the dogs?" Jesus says, referring to her Gentile nature. Her answer stuns everyone, "Even the dogs can eat the crumbs from under the table." I believe Jesus chuckles. All of the miles he had traveled with the disciples had not produced such faith and strength as this woman had just displayed. "Good answer!" Jesus says. And, with that, the woman's daughter is healed.

Jesus' healings of people are not alike. Some are touched by his hand, others by acts of nature, some by those sent by Jesus. None of that happened here. No, this healing took place because a mom would not give up, would not forget her child and would not accept no for an answer. Her boldness saved her daughter's life, and Jesus enjoyed watching it.

God likes bold gestures because he is the author of them. How bold that the God of the universe would become like us so that we could have healing? How bold that God's love would go so far as to die for us in the process?

So, live boldly in this world. Others may not understand it, but our hearts will.

Growing Deeper

Prayer: Gracious God, thank you so much for being bold in this world and for calling us to be bold as well. Help me to live my faith with such purpose and focus that everyone will see You in me. Amen.

Journal Focus: List those ways that you can boldly live your faith in the world. Prioritize them in a schedule that you can follow and accomplish.

To Consider...

What is your definition of bold? Is it a matter of perspective? Seeing or even talking to a doctor at his/her office is often a pain—and I'm not talking about the injection kind of pain. I know it is very frustrating for a mom to wait one hour for a check-up or even several hours for a phone call to be returned.

If you come to my office you will first see the receptionist, then my nurse, then me. But, if you happen to be sitting in the waiting room when three kids come bounding in, wave at the receptionist, tell my nurse "Hi," and walk straight into my office, you probably would say, "What bold kids." But they do not see their actions as bold at all. They are just coming by to talk to their dad (and often to ask for something). They have been told that it is ok to do so—anytime, for any reason.

God has told us to do the same—anytime for any reason. I love for my kids to come by the office. It makes me feel special. It makes us love each other more. I think that's true for God, too. He loves to see us, to hear us tell Him we love Him, and believe it or not, for us to ask Him for things. Is that being bold? I don't think so—we're His kids.

> "Let us then approach the throne of grace with confidence so that we may receive mercy and grace to help us in our time of need."
>
> Hebrews 4:16

Devotion Eighteen: Witness...

To a Forgiven Heart

"Father, Forgive them for they know not what they do....."

Luke 23:34

Just off the hustle and bustle of fast paced Hwy. 49 in south Mississippi sits an important community to me. Seminary, MS is a very small town. Main Street is a collection of diners, gas stations, and memories of days gone by. The local school is the central expression of its existence, fulfilling the duties not only of educating its children, but also of providing a majority of the town's social outlets.

The people are *good* people, who attend one of the many churches within the community; and they are notoriously kind to each other. The pace is slow, and people like it that way. Seminary, MS is a good place to watch life.

My connection to Seminary is unique. I did not grow up there, do not have family who live there, and I have never spent more than two hours within the city limits. However, this community played an important part in my life and helped shape my ministry.

Our stories crossed paths in 1994. I was finishing theology school at Duke University and was preparing to take my first full-time appointment in the United Methodist Church. Seminary UMC was preparing for a new pastor. Both of us were excited and a touch nervous about new beginnings.

The rumor hit on a Sunday morning. Talk had it that the new pastor was HIV positive. Apparently, although it was not a secret, the District Superintendent had thought it wise to not share this information with the congregation. The rumor made its way to the governing board. After a day full of debate and questions, the Administrative Board of Seminary UMC voted not to accept their new pastor.

On Monday, I drove from North Carolina to Hattiesburg, unaware of what had taken place. My covenant meeting was scheduled for Tuesday evening. This is the traditional first meeting between a church and its new pastor. When I arrived at my parents house in Hattiesburg, I received the news from my wife who had been informed by the District Superintendent earlier in the day. We were shocked, hurt, and disappointed. But, it was also one of the most intimate moments in my marriage. We shared our concerns about the future and trusted God together.

The next day, the Bishop asked me to attend the planned covenant meeting. He clearly did not expect me to be appointed as pastor; but, as he stated later, he felt I needed to go for the integrity of the process. Although this was a difficult decision, I agreed and went. The meeting was uncomfortable at best. Those who decided to attend expressed sadness and dismay at the situation. The majority of my opposition was not present. As I sat there, what had begun as discomfort, confusion and anger, quickly turned into compassion as I came face to face with the family of God in crisis. Not just crisis over the appointment of a pastor, but a crisis of the soul. Oh, how they wanted it to be different, but they were so unprepared to make it so. I left that meeting one hour later, convinced that I had just witnessed one of saddest experiences of my life. Not a day has gone by that I haven't prayed for those people and for the veil that fell on their hearts in that moment.

I can only imagine what Jesus felt when he looked out at his brothers and sisters in the faith and realized that they just didn't get it. The sermons, the hope, and all of the promise dwindled in the face of such misguided intentions. His only recourse was to utter, "Forgive them for they do not understand."

But, don't those words make all of us accountable and responsible. I have certainly missed the mark myself, failing to see God at work, or worse yet, seeing His work and not responding. And, still God looks and forgives——no matter what.

As I mentioned earlier, I have spent two hours in Seminary, MS. The first was in 1994; the second was several years later. While driving from Jackson, I suddenly found myself turning off of the highway and at the door of Seminary UMC. I sat there for an hour watching the church and the community as it went by. It was a peaceful moment. I thanked God for what I had been through and for life's little lessons. And... I thanked him for Jesus—who watches us, in spite of our failures and flaws, takes us by the hand, and calls us his own. And...because of Jesus, I realized that Seminary is my community too (whether we like it or not).

Growing Deeper

Prayer: God of forgiveness, thank you for grace and for the power of Your forgiveness in my life. Help me to not only live as one who is forgiven, but to share that forgiveness with others in my life. Amen.

Journal Focus: List those from whom you need to seek forgiveness and those to whom you need to offer forgiveness. Resolve yourself to do it.

To Consider...

Jesus told us to forgive others so *we* could experience true forgiveness. Not forgiving others causes bitterness that clogs up the system of God's work in our lives. So, how did Jesus look down from that cross at the guy holding the hammer and say

"Father, forgive him."? I think He realized several things. First, *that* man was not the enemy. The real enemy was Satan who was trying to destroy God's plan of redemption. Secondly, Jesus realized *that* man had needs and hurts; and, because of His great love, He thought of him first. Third, as it states in Hebrews 12, Jesus endured the cross for the joy set before Him. I think He could look beyond the present situation and its pain to what God had promised—a seat beside Him in Heaven.

Now, let me tell you the rest of Shane's story. He was eventually appointed to his present church—Asbury UMC. They have done much more than just "accept him in spite of his condition." They have made him their own. His place in that church, in the community, is rock solid.

But, you see, Shane had to die on that cross at Seminary and forgive those who put him there—really at no fault of their own. To be Jesus' true disciple, we must die to self on the cross God gives us so that we can be raised to live the life for which He has restored us. All of us have a Seminary—find God there.

> "If anyone would come after me, he must deny himself and take up his cross daily and follow me."
>
> Luke 9:23

Devotion Nineteen:
Witness…

To a Redeemed Life

"Then the Devil came and said, "If you are the Son of God, change these stones into loaves of bread." But Jesus told him, "No! The Scriptures says, 'People need more than bread for their life; they must feed on every word of God.'"

Matthew 4: 3-4

Marina Abramovic is a visual artist. A native of Great Britain, Ms. Abramovic is known around the world for her powerful, living impressions of life and its issues. Some call her exhibits profound; others call them strange. Either way, Ms. Abramovic's work leaves an indelible impression on every one she meets.

Her latest project is a visual fast. In this twelve-day exhibit at the Sean Kelly Gallery in New York City, Ms. Abramovic will live in a 5.5 by 9 foot cage that is wall-to-wall knives. The cage will sit six feet off the ground and will have no facilities or escape. Ms. Abramovic will not talk, eat, read or write. She will live completely and wholly in this box, bordered by a watching world. With a wood plank for her bed and piece of rose quartz for a pillow, Ms. Abramovic will be at the mercy of her emotions and stamina.

When asked by the *New York Times* why she was doing this, Ms. Abramovic stated that the project symbolized the dramatic changes in American life since September 11, 2001. "The whole idea of time," Ms. Abramovic continued, "of what can happen in the next second, came to Americans in a way we know very well, very sadly in Europe. And this piece will be about living in the moment, in the absolute here and now." (1) The *Times* piece went on to praise Ms. Abramovic's work as "balancing sensationalism with a deep sense of purpose." After reading about it, one has to applaud its originality and bravery.

But, it is not really original. Ms. Abramovic's premise is that life cannot be meaningful without an insightful sense of time or without an element of sacrifice attached to it. Her dramatic interpretation of life begs the question, "Can life, void of the trappings, be made meaningful?" I believe Ms. Abramovic is actually talking about redemption.

A colleague of mine once defined redemption as being "brought back from the edge of nothingness." In a world that so often attempts to create significance from the mundane, material items of life, can nothingness be overcome by meaning? Jesus says, "Yes."

Jesus' journey to the wilderness reminds us that life requires self-sacrifice at times. "If you are the son of God," the Devil taunts, "Then turn these stones into bread." Why shouldn't Jesus do it? But, Jesus knows the deeper meaning of Satan's question. "Don't you trust your Father?" "Would a loving God send you out here to be hungry?" "In a world of plenty, why do you have to starve?" The questions keep ringing.

How did Jesus respond? "People need more than bread...." They need purpose, presence and confirmation that this dance of life has some spiritual rhythm to it. Truth is, Jesus knows that we are already living in boxes, bordered by a watching world—the boxes of success, bad relationships, a world gone mad—and we want out. So, Jesus escapes it all, trusts in the Father, and teaches us a lesson about the real "here and now." A place where scared, hurting people can sit down, take some rest and find perspective. In the process, He draws us back from the nothingness and unveils a life that means more than we can ever imagine.

Growing Deeper

Prayer: God of grace, thank you for the wildernesses of our lives that we might learn how to depend on You. Help me to tear down the "boxes" and to find meaning in every aspect of life. Amen.

Journal Focus: List those areas of your life where God is seeking to teach meaning and purpose in your life. How can you change your response and focus in each of these areas?

To Consider...

What is a Christian's greatest witness to the world? Why should someone want to become a Christian? Are we any different? Does the world see something in us that they would want in their life? I often think not! Why? How? I think it is because we try to "live on bread alone," and we spiritually starve.

I know many Christians who painfully toil through the week, just trying to make it from Sunday to Sunday to receive their spiritual food. They try *the feast and famine* spiritual diet plan. I don't believe that plan works well for the truly restored Christian. Since we are often compared to sheep, we should spiritually eat like sheep—grazing all the time. Yes, sometimes with big meals but, always nibbling on the green grass.

Jesus knew that we would need many of the things the world needs. In fact He said that His Father would supply them in Matthew 6:32 &33. But, He said to first go after the kingdom of God and then your life will be right—right with God and right with the world. Then the world will see a difference. They will see someone who is grounded in the truth of God's word, not the selfishness of the world. They will see real contentment with life and will stop at nothing to share that with others.

Devotion Twenty: Witness...

To a Restored Images

"When you become a Christian you are a new person."

2 Corinthians 5: 17

"Seek God and live."

Amos 5: 4

In today's world, computers provide for just about everything. Financial information, personal statistics, payrolls, and gas pumps are a few of the items for which computers play a significant role. One cannot be born or die in this world without a computer's influence. Every sermon that I have written in the last five years is catalogued on a computer. On a trip to Gulf Shores, Alabama, Pokey, the girls and I posed for pictures on the beach. No more paper proofs—they were viewed via the Internet.

In the movie, *The Net*, Sandra Bullock plays a character whose identity was destroyed simply by tampering with computers. The entire movie is one woman's search to restore her identity. In the information age, the information oftentimes controls the informer. It is sad when the tree is swinging the monkey.

Recently, the crash of my computer hard drive placed my world on pause. My anxiety and sadness resonated throughout every portal of my existence. (That is a fancy way of saying that I was in a really bad mood, and everyone paid the price.) A friend was able to get the computer running again and to save my data. How did he do it? By restoring the original saved information.

A couple of points struck me about this process. First you don't "save" new information; you save the original. Second, it is from this process that information might be restored, not to newness, but to an original form. Computer operators do not want new information when their hard drives collapse; they want their original information. Why? Because, the original information is an imprint of its creation. You can never have a "new" original.

In the above Scripture, Paul tells the church at Corinth that when we become Christians, we are "new" people. Most read this and understand it as a discarding of the old. Such a concept, in my opinion, has led to a devaluing of life and of the power of a creator to retain vestiges of good in His creation even in the midst of our sin.

In my opinion, what Paul means is not *new* in reference to the original, but in reference to the present life one lives. If this is the case, then what Paul is talking about is really restoration not just making new.

The early Church used a phrase in Latin called *Imago Dia* to describe the creation of humanity in the *image* of God. Most great pieces of religious art contain references to this original state of humanity; and, as we read in Genesis 2, God considered it "very good." The goodness disappears during the fall in Genesis 3 when Adam and Eve's image becomes confused by self-will. The serpent convinced them to tamper with the original—to provide a little "spiritual editing" if you please. But that didn't mean the original was gone, just distorted.

I have often heard preachers talk about "dying to self" as though some type of spiritual suicide must take place. Personally, I prefer the translation that calls this process a "stripping away" of our old life, so that we might see the original underneath. There is too much goodness in this world for it all to be intrinsically bad. Just watch a group of preschoolers picking flowers, and you will be convinced that there are still glimpses all around of what we were created to be.

In my life, I don't necessarily want to be made new; I want to be made His and what He has intended for me to be from the beginning. How do we do that? The prophet Amos gives us some good advice, "Seek God and live."

Growing Deeper

Prayer: Gracious God, thank you so much for sending Jesus that I might be restored to what You created me to be. Help me to become Yours completely in everything that I am and in everything that I do. Amen.

Journal Focus: If you awakened tomorrow and everything was perfect, how would your world look? What do you need from God in order to either change your world or live bravely in the midst of it?

To Consider...

Saint Augustine said, "Love God and do what you want." When I first heard that quote I thought, "Whoa, that will never work, there's too much of the 'what you want' in me." Then I realized that the more you love God, the more your will becomes what His will already is for you. As you love Him more, you want to be like Him—restored to His image.

I am told that a man who once took rough tree limbs and carved them into an almost perfect image of a dog was asked, "How do you do that?" He reportedly said, "I just take away everything that doesn't look like a dog."

I think that is what God does in our restoration. He takes away areas of our lives that do not look like His image. Sometimes He uses a deep spiritual moment; often times He uses a "crash of the system." But we are promised that He uses "all things" in Romans 8:28&29.

Trust God that He loves you with a love beyond description. Trust Him that He is working to give you life beyond compare. Trust Him—love Him—and do what you want.

"Now to Him who is able to do immeasurably more than all we ask or imagine, according to His power that is at work within us, to Him be glory in the church and in Christ Jesus throughout all generations, for ever and ever! Amen."

(Ephesians 3: 20-21).

Devotion Twenty-one: Witness...

To an Unseen Hope

"So be truly glad! There is a wonderful joy ahead, even though it is necessary for you to endure many trials for a while..."
"You love him even though you have never seen him. Though you do not see him, you trust him; and even now you are happy with a glorious, inexpressible joy. Your reward for trusting him will be the salvation of your souls."
1 Peter 1: 6, 8-9

Bill had been in the hospital for nearly two months when I met him. A small gentleman in his early 80's, Bill had been diagnosed with cancer three months earlier, and the disease had spread rapidly. He had been in and out of various experimental treatments, but none had been successful. The doctors were preparing Bill and his family for Hospice care. They said the end should come in 6 to 8 weeks.

A friend asked me to visit Bill in the hospital. Unsure of what to expect, I was delighted to find a wonderful man who was very alert and aware of his surroundings. The cancer had taken its toll on his body, but his mind was as sharp as ever. I would visit Bill every week for the next month. Although he was increasingly in pain, Bill never complained about his condition. Instead, he talked about three subjects: the war, his wife and his faith.

Bill's wife, Dot, had died two years prior to his sickness. She had been the light of his life. When he talked about her, you could sense how much he loved her, and how much he missed her. They had been married for "57 wonderful years" he would always say, and, then, with a smirk, he would add, "Well, at least 39 of them were." Bill said that Dot was a great cook and an even better kisser. Oh, how he would have traded everything for an apple pie and a "smooch," as he would call it.

Bill was also a veteran. A Navy man, Bill had served in both the Atlantic and Pacific theaters during World War II. In fact, he was at the battle of Lahti Gulf, still considered one of the greatest naval battles of all time. Bill loved the Navy and every-thing about it—the uniforms, the ships and the smell of the water. When he talked about the war, Bill was transformed from an ailing 82 year old man into a young fighting machine again.

However, Bill's favorite topic was his faith in God. He told me that he had accepted Christ as his Savior as a 12 year old boy. He was visiting his grandparents, and he was attending revival at the local Baptist church. "I didn't pay attention much," he would say. "I only went because of Maggie Mae Bronson, the cute little red head who sat on the second pew." He would always get a glimmer when he thought of Maggie Mae. "Then, one night, it hit me. The preacher was talking about sin and Jesus, and before I knew it, I was walking the aisle." Bill would always pause and add, "It was a long walk from the back pew." Bill was baptized in a local creek on a hot summer day. "I came out of that water," Bill said, "and, I have been walking with Jesus ever since."

I had heard such professions before, but with Bill I believed it. Here was a man who loved life, his family and his God. He wasn't ashamed to proclaim his faith or to talk about his disappointments. His life had not been easy. He and Dot had lost a young child to cancer. Bill's younger brother was killed in a train accident. And, at age 47, Bill and Dot lost everything in a house fire. But, in the midst of it, Bill never lost hope that the God who had pushed him into the aisle at age 12 would never forsake him.

That thought was especially poignant during my last days with Bill. As he lay dying, I watched first-hand as a man of God became a saint. One day while I was with him, the doctor came by and asked Bill how he was doing. "I am ready to go home, Doc,"

Bill answered. The doctor replied with a few words about Hospice and its program. But, as I looked at him, I knew what Bill meant. "Not that home, Doc. The real home where my Dot and my Jesus live." The doctor didn't know what to say.

Bill went home the next day. Emotion surged through me when I heard of his death. Why had such a good man suffered so much pain and loss in his life? Why were his last days so difficult? The questions made me pause and wonder where was God in all of this? Was there possibly any redeeming factor? I had asked these questions before during the death of a very close friend. Can God make sense of such insensible situations?

The apostle Peter states that it is necessary to endure the trials of this world in order to experience the joy of the next. However, through Bill's life and death, I realized that the power of perseverance is not simply in the endurance of trial, but by experiencing joy *now* in spite of it. What was Bill's testimony? That he had survived? No! His testimony was that beyond every disappointment and tear, he had not lost his joy. Bill's joy rested not in the physical existence of this world, but deeper in his soul. How can someone go through so many inexplicable circumstances in this world and still proclaim joy? I have come to realize that it is because their eyes are focused on that which the world cannot see.

Not long after Bill's death, on a trip to the coast, I pulled over at a local state park and stood on a creek bank. I wondered if this creek bank was similar to the one Bill had seen the day he was baptized. I wondered if the noise of the running water was the same or if the breeze was familiar. And... I wondered if the people baptized here were as sure of their faith as Bill was.

Oh, Bill loved Jesus all right, that much was certain. And now, it all made sense—the struggles, the loss, the cancer—for he was getting to see Him face to face. Indeed, what a glorious, inexpressible joy—now and then! Thanks Bill.

Growing Deeper

Prayer: God of compassion and joy, thank you for the Bills of this world who remind us of Your love and grace. Help me to live my faith with certainty and purpose that others might see the inexpressible joy that is You. Amen.

Journal Focus: List those areas in your life where you need to be thankful and aware of God's presence. How do you specifically celebrate what God is doing in and around you today?

To Consider...

Why does that plum tree have plums in the summer? Because plums are really in the tree all the time, they just come out at the right time—or in due time. If you are a Christian, you have joy in you all the time—it is a fruit of God's Holy Spirit in you. You don't muster it up; you don't earn it; you don't "faith it"— it is just there like the ability to produce is in a fruit tree from the moment it sprouts from a seed.

I think the problem is that some of us feel like we should experience that deep sense of joy at all times, but that's called Heaven. Life is tough sometimes, and I, like everyone, struggle to know the joy when it is. I do know the peace of God's presence, the contentment that He is there and that He has a plan. But, in James 1:2, all He has asked me to do is "consider it pure joy" because of His promise to work in me through the tough times. He has promised that the joy is there and it will be evident in due season.

> "May the God of hope fill you with all joy and peace as you trust in Him, so that you may overflow with hope by the power of the Holy Spirit."
>
> Romans 15:13

Section Four

Worship

Celebrating God's Presence

Luke 1: 26-38

Romans 16: 25-27

Devotion Twenty-two:
Worship...

Because He is Worthy

"Great is the Lord! He is most worthy of praise! He is to be revered above all things."

Psalm 96: 4

Ida Mae Jackson was the bomb, at least in the sleepy, small South Mississippi town where my best friend's grandparents lived. She was the sixteen-year-old daughter of the mayor. Ida Mae was medium height with auburn hair and big blue eyes. She was "Miss" everything, and everyone loved her. In fact, Ms. Jackson's position in town, along with her charming good looks, made her a favorite at every civic event. For Ida Mae was not just pretty to look at, she was a performer.

Ida Mae's talent was vocal performance. She had taken lessons since the second grade, and, according to her daddy, was going to be a big star one-day. Her forte was special music at the local churches. Now, one needs to understand that, in small town Mississippi, "special music" can indeed be, well... special. I have seen it all when it comes to those precious moments just prior to the sermon when some well-meaning soul belts out notes as though the very stability of Heaven itself depended on it. My personal favorite was "It is well with my soul" played entirely on harmonica. Point being, *special* does not always equal *good*.

Every summer, I would go with my friend to his grandparents' house for a weekend. His grandmother, Memee, would spoil us rotten. The woman cooked like Julia Child (but with food that you would eat). She loved having company, and she loved taking people to church.

The news on this particular weekend trip was that Ida Mae was going to be the special music during worship on Sunday at Memee's church. Now, I had personally never met Ida Mae, but I had seen her in a parade riding on one of the many floats. I am not for sure, but I believe that she was "Harvest Queen" or something. Anyway... needless to say, church took on a whole new importance to a pair of fourteen-year-old boys when they learned that, for one brief moment, the usually dull worship service would be transformed into an experience of beauty.

We arrived at church early (to get a good seat of

course). The church was at the end of Church Road (no lie) and stood next to a large pasture and a barn. The family of the couple who owned the house next door had donated the land for the church sometime right after dirt was given its name. (Another rule about small town churches—everything, and I mean everything, has been donated by somebody!)

The service began as the pastor and the choir made their way to the chancel area. Ida Mae and her parents came in a few seconds late—a grand and beautiful entrance if you ask me. We sang three hymns (very slowly), prayed and took up an offering. Then, the pastor got up and introduced our special music. Ida Mae stood and smiled. She took the microphone from the podium, said a few words of thanks for allowing her to be there, and began to sing.

What I experienced next was very confusing. How could something so horrible emit from something so beautiful? It was like the first time you realize that your first-born baby's "poop" stinks—you are unprepared for the emotional roller coaster that you are flailing on. No one had bothered to mention that, along with the beauty and legend that was Ida Mae Jackson, the girl could not sing a lick. It was like a Twilight Zone episode; everyone is sitting there smiling while Ida Mae tears "Father's Eyes" (that was the song) to pieces.

To make matters worse, a mule in the neighbor's barn joined in as well. Every time Ida Mae would hit a high note, the mule would sing with her.

Finally, mercifully, the song (whose author must have envisioned a moment like this) stopped, and Ida Mae smiled beautifully as the congregation shouted, "Amen!" (No one dare clap in a small town Baptist church.) The whole experience reminded me of the statement, "I ain't smiling cause it was good; I'm smiling cause its over."

However, I will always remember Ida Mae's "special" music because she sang it like she meant it. After all, she wasn't singing to a longhaired fourteen-year-old boy, but to God. I believe the Psalmist understood about special music. I am sure that more than one well-meaning shepherd had butchered a religious song on a harp before, but the Psalmist doesn't seem to mind. "Great is the Lord!" he says. "He is worthy!" And, that is the heart of our worship—bad notes and all.

Don't get me wrong, I never went to hear Ida Mae sing again, but I do remember the look on her face when she finished. It looked like she and Jesus were entirely by themselves, and— beyond all explanation— he was pleased.

My three year old began singing the other day, and I was reminded of Ida Mae (for more than one reason). Like Ida Mae Jackson, Juli Anna has big blue eyes, and she can't sing a lick. But, she worships God, and He likes it.

Growing Deeper

Prayer: God of Praise, thank you for the privilege of worshipping You and for being with brothers and sisters while we worship. Help me to appreciate the power of worship and being together with You. Amen.

Journal Focus: List ways that you can worship God today through your actions, your service and your attitude.

To Consider...

In "For the Love of the Game" Kevin Costner's key to success as a major league pitcher is dependent on his ability to "clear the mechanism" and focus on the moment, not the many distractions around him. We should strive to do the same in worship. As we enter God's presence, so many competing forces are present. Satan hates it when we give glory to God. Those around us compete for our attention. And, unfortunately, our own selfish desires rear up their ugly heads. But... we must work at clearing the mechanism because it is all about God and who He is. When we are able to do this, worship takes on a whole new meaning. As we fellowship, it is all about God's unique Spirit as He moves in and through those around us. As we sing, the beauty of the music is not in who is singing but to whom the song is offered. As we pray, we are able to see the very heart of God. As we give, we share in the expanse of His Kingdom. As we listen to His word proclaimed, we are set free. And... as we go from that time of worship, we carry Jesus to a world that desperately needs to know Him.

> "Command those ... to put their hope in God, who richly provides us with everything for our enjoyment.... In this way they will lay up treasure for themselves as

a firm foundation for the coming age, so that they may take hold of the life that is truly life."

(1 Timothy 6:17-19)

Devotion Twenty-three:
Worship...

Because He Always Answers

"When I pray, you answer me; you encourage me by giving me the strength I need."

Psalm 138: 3

The sign read, "Please turn off all cell phones and beepers at the door." The man leading the workshop believed that mobile communication devices were destroying the world, and, especially, his presentations. He was a self-help guru, pronounced by many as one the experts on personal success and achievement. His seminars were in great demand, and people paid large amounts of money to attend.

One look and it was apparent that he liked himself very much. But, people paid the money, and he gave them the "show for success."

Therefore, *guru man* was not amused when the cell phone rang. It belonged to a young woman sitting in the back. She grabbed it as fast as she could, but it had already been ringing for some time before she found it deep inside her purse. The young woman tried to leave before answering, but before she made it out of the room, everyone could hear, "Yes, honey, what is it?"

When she arrived back at her seat, *guru man* stopped his normal talk and said, "For the young woman in the back, if your future success is not more important than a cell phone call, maybe you are in the wrong seminar." The young woman, horribly embarrassed and with tears in her eyes, collected her things and left. *Guru man* continued his presentation.

Several weeks later, the workshop leader recounted his experience to a group of college professors attending a national conference. He was facilitating a workshop on personal success. He was proud of how he had *established some order* in his presentation and, through the example of the young woman, taught the whole room a valuable lesson. As he continued to relate the encounter, a young professor spoke from across the table, "How do you know that it wasn't her sick child from home calling to talk with mom? What if the young woman was a single mom who *really* was trying to better herself, but didn't have enough money to attend your seminar and get a baby sitter at the same time? What if that cell phone was her key to doing better, and, dare I say it, to a little peace of mind? What if, by your humiliation of her, you shut the door on her future?"

"Who are you?" the stunned *guru man* asked. "My name is Dr. Pokey Stanford," the woman answered. "At home I have two small children and a husband who everyday fights for his life. I keep my cell phone turned on, and when it rings, I answer it." Dr. Stanford continued, "Because when the people I love need me, no smooth talking know it all in a $700 Italian suit is going to keep me from responding. And... I think *that* is a successful life."

"When the people I love need me...." What a powerful statement! The Psalmist tells us that when we call, God answers—no call waiting and no signs at the door. He is more willing to respond than we are to call, but still He is available and waiting for our request. The power of worship is found in this truth—God never closes the connection between Himself and His children. When we are afraid, in trouble or just needing to hear a kind voice, He is present.

Jesus says that the Holy Spirit comes as means of mobile communication whereby the children of God can always feel Him near. It is our open line, the cell phone that's never turned off.

Worship today can be too linear and way too ordered. Many believe that by attending a "program" of worship, one fulfills the duty for spiritual success. Worship is more than that. It is about connection and hearing God's voice. Worship inspires, yes, but it also soothes and comforts. It is certainly not one dimensional, whereby one person stands and imbues wisdom. No, it is about the person sitting next to us, about the spirit in the air, and about the needs that we all bring. And... worship is about calling out and knowing that someone will answer.

In 1998, I lost a dear friend to a sudden illness. Not only was Nancy one of my closest friends, she was also my doctor. We had built a close and powerful relationship. I cannot remember a time when I needed advice, guidance or just to talk that I couldn't pick up the phone and talk with her. She was always available. Her death was very sudden. I assisted at the funeral and helped her family cope with the loss. However, I didn't fully realize my own loss until that first time I picked up the phone to give her a call. My mind knew that she wouldn't answer, but someone forgot to tell my heart.

How good it is to know that God always answers. Even the best of friends may one day leave us for a while, but God never will.

Growing Deeper

Prayer: God of grace, thank you for always being present when I need You, but also for being near when I think I don't. Help me realize Your presence in my life and celebrate that presence by worshipping through my actions and life today. Amen.

Journal Focus: List those people in our lives that need for you to be God's connection to them. How can you reach out to them and provide comfort and guidance today?

To Consider...

What *is* the purpose of worship? Why do we attend a "worship service" each week? If the most important reason we attend is to be inspired, we probably won't be.

If the most important reason is to tell God how much we love Him and to praise Him corporately, we will do that. In the process, not only will we be successful, we'll be changed.

Worship should bring out the very best in all of us. When we gather together to worship, we are one with each other and with God's Spirit as we celebrate who God is.

In Philippians 4, Paul tells us to rejoice always. That's what worship is all about— "re-joying" who God is and what He is about in our lives. Just like a tire must be retread, I need to be "re-joyed." Our gentleness should be obvious to all because we know that God is near us all the time. Because He is near, He knows us. He knows our needs; He knows our fears; and He knows us better than we know ourselves—yet He loves us. He wants us to know His peace as a very active part of our lives – not something that moves in as all care is removed, but something that fights away our anxious thoughts to keep us in the very presence of God.

And so the circle is complete. God reached down to us, so we know Him, so we worship Him. We worship Him, and He is able to inhabit us even more.

> "For from Him and through Him and to Him are all things. To Him be the glory forever! Amen."
>
> (Romans 11:36)

Devotion Twenty-four:
Worship...

Because He gives us a Common Story

"It was by faith that the people of Israel marched around Jericho seven days, and the walls came crashing down."
Hebrews 11: 30

Have you ever watched children at a birthday party? When allowed to just be themselves, children transform any room, playground or gymnasium into a fantasy world of castles and exciting adventures. They talk, run, laugh, cry and fuss. But... through it all, they live life fully and drain every drop from the moment. They have a common thread that runs through them: they are children, and children, as though they know it will not last forever, squeeze a full portion of existence from every tear and giggle, all the while, I am convinced, wondering if mom and dad standing on the wall could ever have experienced such things.

Don't you believe it? Watch your children at a public playground. My daughter can play for five minutes on a field full of strangers and will return with the best friend she has ever had in the world. It happens without fail, much to dad's chagrin. Children do not fathom the evil of this world until they are taught or shown it. Which makes me ask, "Should they ever really need to know?" The answer, of course, is "yes", but why? If no child were exposed to abuse, abandonment or acts of violence, would the world they grow up in be the same? Could we change the world by tapping into the common story of childhood, instead of making every child grow up and take on the overgrown bravado of adults?

Our narrative consumes childhood, and it consumes our faith as well. The reason that most people reflect on their childhood with fondness and can share that openly with those whom they have never met is because we all share those moments— of being king, princess or pirate. In a world of such emotional corruption, it was our Camelot—the place and time when things seemed as they should be.

In the passage above, and throughout all of Hebrews 11, God makes sense of the journey and, once again, gives us a common story. From the beginning of time until Christ's return, God's plan interweaves through human existence, and, in the process, an unsuspecting shepherd in the 9th century B.C. is intimately connected to fishermen after the turn of the millennium. The struggles, failures and fears give way in knowing that there was some purpose behind it all. I can only imagine what Heaven is like when a new "child" comes home, and all of God's people sit and tell the story. Maybe Moses is the first to applaud and agree, while Elijah shouts an "Amen." Does Peter nudge Abraham as he nods the old "been there" nod? Does David look at Jeremiah and wink? And, does Jeremiah growl back? (Poor Jeremiah...) What a picture this must be! And, best of all, we are a part of it—Now!

I believe that every time the family of God gathers to worship, the story of spiritual childhood should come to life. We sing, speak and pray the words of our spiritual ancestors (maybe not in the same style, but with the same heart), and for that moment, a simple room or gymnasium is transformed into a temple and complete strangers become best friends.

And... when I see my children playing and just being children, I watch for the glimmer in my own soul and wonder what it would be like to be transported to their world where paychecks and appointments do not matter. Oh, how many times I have wanted to jump into Juli Anna's Doodle Bug electric car and hit the open road. But, knowing that Juli Anna would tell me that I am too big, I stand there and chuckle realizing that I am connected to my children by more than just parenthood, but my childhood as well. And... I smile.

How pleased God must be around that Heavenly campfire, and in every moment that the Church gathers when His children realize how they are connected—how they were never truly alone, forsaken or abandoned, and how in the end, it all meant something. I believe that God stands there as a proud parent watching the proverbial lights go on, nudges Jesus, and... smiles.

Growing Deeper

Prayer: God of community, thank you for calling your children together and for expecting us to work together in service to You. Help me to faithfully care for my brothers and sisters as we walk the journey of faith together. Amen.

Journal Focus: List those opportunities in your life where you can join with others to serve and worship.

To Consider...

Do you attend "their" church or do you attend "your" church? I heard someone say that one easy way to tell is if you will pick up a piece of paper off the floor and throw it in the trash! I believe it is critical that we attend *our* church, but how do we feel a part of the family? By working together for the common good seems an obvious answer.

In Ephesians 4, Paul talks about using our spiritual gifts to help each other in "attaining to the whole measure of the fullness of Christ." Wow!

What a church it would be if we all were striving to be full of Christ and our worship reflected that.

We need each other to be all that we can be. Sure, you can and should have a private worship service at times – just you and God. And it can be very special. But to live the Christian life as it should be lived, to accomplish what God wants to accomplish in and through us, and to really experience God completely, we must worship...together as family.

> "And let us consider how we may spur one another on toward love and good deeds. Let us not give up meeting together, as some are in the habit of doing, but let us encourage one another."
>
> (Hebrews 10:24-25)

Devotion Twenty-five:
Worship

Because He Believes in Miracles

"For a child is born to us, a son is given to us. And the government will rest on his shoulders. These will be his royal titles: Wonderful Counselor, Mighty God, Everlasting Father, Prince of Peace. His ever expanding, peaceful government will never end. He will rule forever with fairness and justice from the throne of his ancestor David. The passionate commitment of the Lord Almighty will guarantee this!"

Isaiah 9: 6-7

I met Jack at the Cincinnati/Northern Kentucky airport. We were both waiting for the Delta connection. I was going home after a speaking engagement in North Carolina. "I build things," was Jack's reply when I asked what he did for a living. It was an unusual question for me. I am not the type of traveler who likes chit-chat or necessarily meeting new friends. But, for some reason on this day, I decided to "crossover."

Jack was a pleasant guy, who looked to be in his early forties, although the strain and stress of travel made us both feel much older. His most distinctive feature was that his right eye was a darker shade of blue than the other. I don't suppose that this was normally evident except that, on this particular day, Jack was wearing a deep blue shirt that accentuated the difference.

Even though he did not ask for a reply, I said, "I am a minister." The look on his face was priceless. You could tell that he expected me to whip out a copy of the "Four Spiritual Laws" or, goodness forbid, the Bible, stand in one of the terminal chairs and begin preaching. (I love to do this to people!) His expression screamed, "Please don't say anything else! Freak!"

Realizing that I had just become John Candy's character in the movie, *Planes, Trains, and Automobiles*, I backed off and said, "Sorry to be so forward, I am just ready to pass the time and see my family." "Do you have children?" Jack asked after a few moments of silence. "One daughter and one on the way" I replied. "I have three children... well, I *had* three children," Jack said quietly.

These are the moments when any good teacher, guide or therapist will "capture the silence." You really don't have to say anything, because something is about to happen.

"I'm gone a lot, you know, with my work and all," Jack said. "My wife couldn't handle it. I look back on it now, and I know that it was my fault, but I was so angry that I didn't do anything about it—and then, I looked up and we were divorced." Jack paused, and, for the first time, looked me in the eyes. "She moved across the country. I haven't seen her or the children in some time. I've wanted to call, but I don't know what to say. She's been so angry, and I can only imagine what the girls think." Jack stopped talking and looked away.

After a few seconds, I asked inquisitively, "I'm sorry. Do you still love her?" "I don't know," Jack said quickly. But, I could tell that he *did* know, and that was killing him. "I think you do know," I said, without really considering the possibilities, "And I think that you want to pick up a phone and get your family back." Jack with a sense of loss on his face said, "But, they won't come back." "How do you know that?" I said.

By this time in the conversation, I had clearly stepped over the bounds and was treading in dangerous waters. I knew that, at any minute, Jack could leave, and this discussion would be over. But, something kept pressing me forward, and I followed. After several seconds of awkward silence, Jack looked me in the eyes again and said, "It would take a miracle, and I have stopped believing in miracles."

Sometimes, when God opens doors, He does so by providing a small crack that opens softly without much fanfare. Other times, He swings it open with bells and whistles blazing! So, in the Cincinnati Airport, I shared with Jack my miracle story of HIV, blindness and eye surgeries at 16, a beautiful and faithful wife, and two wonderful children. "Not only do I believe in miracles, Jack," I said. "I live one." I asked Jack if I could pray with him for a miracle in his life. "Would you mind?" He said. "No, not at all," I replied, taking him by the hand, "because, Jack, I work for someone who builds things, too." I gave Jack my card, and we went our separate ways.

As I flew home, I reflected on what had just happened. *Our God is amazing.* He is not bound by time, space or personal idiosyncrasies. Some would say it was a coincidence....

But, It was no coincidence that a simple birth in Bethlehem would cause such a stir throughout the kingdom. It was no coincidence that a Carpenter's son would scare the establishment and create disorder. It was no coincidence that what should have been another execution would cause a Roman governor to debate ethics. It was certainly no coincidence that a simple trip to a friend's tomb would change the world. It is not a coincidence that two children of God would meet in the Cincinnati Airport.

And, it is not a coincidence that Jesus is born each day in our lives, through our journeys, our families and through our opportunities to share with the Jacks of this world that miracles still happen. Jack, wherever you are, I am still praying for you, for your family and for that miracle....

Growing Deeper

Prayer: God of new beginnings, we thank you for Jesus who was and is the greatest miracle of all. Help us to live as redeemed and restored people who share the power of that miracle in and through our lives today.

Journal Focus: List your blessings and joys. Take time to describe the miracles in your life. How can you share those miracles with others that they may come to know God's love in Jesus?

To Consider...

Q: Why did the Jews not recognize who Jesus was? A: God's plan.

Q: Why did Jesus have to suffer such a cruel death? A: God's plan.

Q: Why are you who you are today? A: God's plan.

But, you say, I have made some very bad decisions in my life – some poor choices. That's OK. Did God want you to make those poor choices? No. Can God work with you and cause good to come from those choices? Absolutely. That's what Romans 8:28-29 is all about.

Look at the titles Isaiah gave Jesus:

Wonderful Counselor—so who needs a counselor? People who make good choices? No, all of us who mess up and get all gummed up because of it.

Mighty God—why do we need a Mighty God? Because we are so strong? No, because we are so weak and need desperately for someone to take care of us.

Everlasting Father—why everlasting? Because we mess up over and over and over again. I ask myself often, "How can I be so stupid to make such a bad decision again and again. God must be frustrated and ready to give up on me." No He's not – He's everlasting.

Prince of Peace—the best title for me. See I can deal with all of life's ugliness and all of *my* ugliness if I have peace that God is God and He loves me and is in control. I know He can do what I can't do. I know that He can fix what I mess up— because He is God.

Don't waste what Jesus did for you. When He came to earth as a baby He brought Almighty God to *us*! Don't let Satan steal even one moment of life from you. Don't look at life as it is, look at life as God intended for it to be—and live it! And remember, you give your life to God—completely and constantly and He does the rest for "the passionate commitment of the Lord Almighty will *guarantee* this!"

Then you will be SALT AND LIGHT.

Works Cited

Devotion 2

Martindale, Wayne and Jerry Root, editors. *The Quotable Lewis*. Wheaton: Illinois. Tyndale House Publishing, Inc. 1989.

Devotion 5

Dewey, John. *Experience and Education*. New York: MacMillan Publishing. 1938

Devotion 8

Foster, Richard. *Celebration of Discipline*. San Francisco: Harper Collins Publishers. 1988.

Devotion 15

Turner, Steve. "Amazing Grace, How Sweet the Sound." *Good News*. November/December 2002.

Devotion 19

"A Visual Fast." *New York Times*. Sunday, November 10, 2002.

Printed in the United States
25536LVS00001B/1-96